THE
PLAIN
OF
SILVER

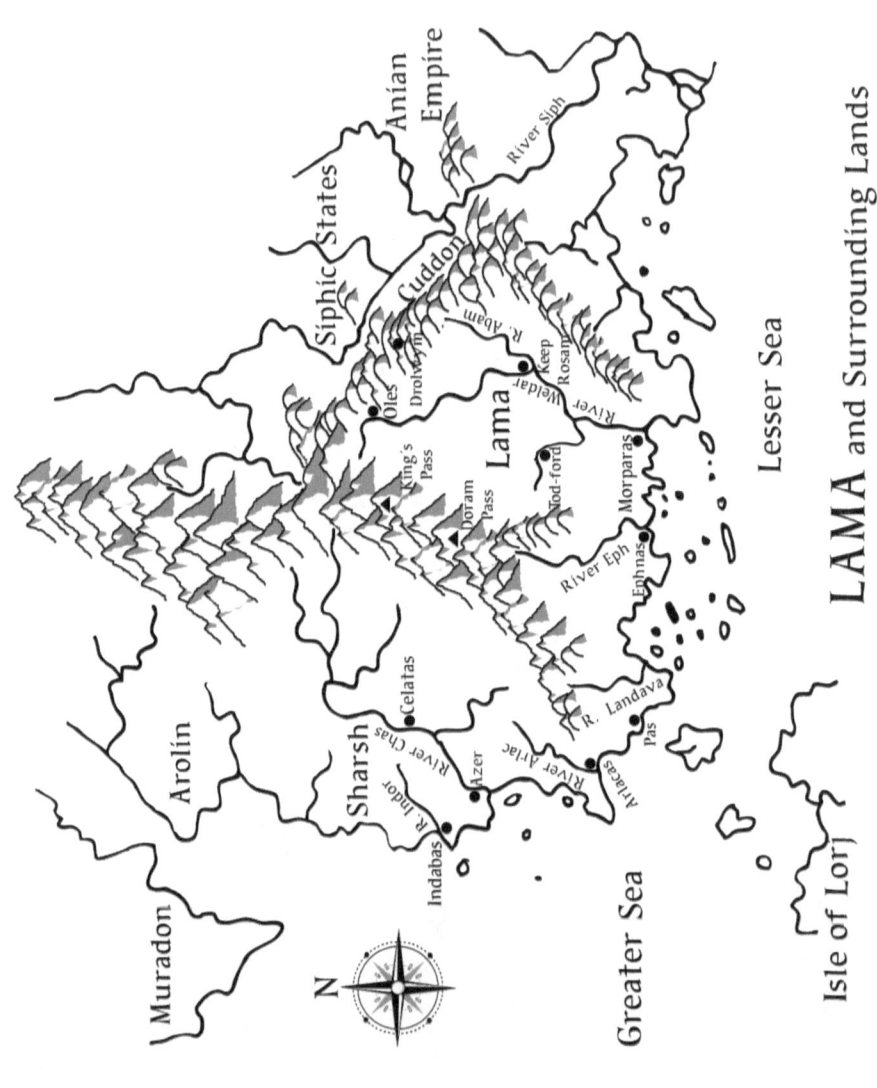

LAMA and Surrounding Lands

THE PLAIN OF SILVER

Stephen Brooke

Arachis Press 2022

They would forge a new destiny for themselves.

The Plain of Silver
©2022 Stephen Brooke

ISBN 978-1-937745-83-7

Arachis Press
4803 Peanut Road
Graceville, FL 32440
http://arachispress.com

OF TRAVELERS: THE FIRST TALE

1

FOR THE CUDDON, it was a fine day. All the more so for being late autumn; the sun turned the perpetual mists to gold where they clung to the rounded hills. In a grave near a little cottage, nestled among the pines, they laid the bard Guesare to rest.

Beside his sister, they laid him to rest. Donzalo had loved them both. He breathed in memories along with the scent of the forest. Here he had tarried a few weeks, less than a year before. Here he would have stayed, lived out a lifetime with Jola, had his destiny not decreed otherwise.

Destiny. He knew not yet whether he believed in it. No matter; Ansa stood now at his side and together they would forge a new destiny for themselves.

"Bards are highly respected in this land, the equals of priests," Oder whispered to his companions. "A sort of priesthood, themselves."

Many had come to pay their respects, to the bard, to the man. Donzalo looked around the circle of mourners. Se, Guesare's mother, was to be expected, and her circle of priestesses, the devotees of the Great Mother, Rema. So, too, his father, Vantare, Thane of Drolwym. The brothers, Mausare and Habidros who had accompanied them from Lama, and Ourru, who had not. A sister, a stout woman named Cuelle, Donzalo had not met before. As Ourru, she did not live near Drolwym and had her own life and family at some distant farmstead.

Mausare's wife, Lanta, stood near him. Their many children were sensibly back at the keep. Young Casurru, cousin to Guesare and heir to Drolwym, seemed particularly downcast. He looked rather like Guesare, didn't he?

Se was praying? Yes, in Krevid, the language of the Cuddon, though most here knew Muram. Oder would certainly understand Krevid; as a master of spies it would be most useful. Jobareth would not.

And Ansa? He knew so little yet of the woman he loved, sister of Oder and a spy herself. If they were to live in these hills, to settle into the abandoned keep of Sabatare, they should both be knowledgeable of the land's language and ways.

Something moved, barely to be noticed, in the shadow of the pines. "Arsel." He mouthed it more than he whispered it, but the fay emerged to stand silently beside the grave for a moment. The graves; he had loved Jola even as had Donzalo.

All was done, Guesare buried, the appropriate words said. Those attending began whispered conversations. Some cast an eye toward the fay but nothing more as he woke from his reverie and turned to Donzalo.

"This is Arsel, a prince of the Fay," spoke the Laman. "My friend."

"And Guesare's," added the elf. He was the height of an average man, but slight of build, with skin the color of snow and pale indigo eyes beneath raven brows and hair.

Jobareth might never have seen an Other of any sort before. As to the Anian brother and sister? Again, Donzalo knew too little of them. "I greet you, Lord Arsel," said Ansa, and abruptly asked, "Can you tell me of Fachalana?"

"And Sir Blen?" added Jobareth Nafal.

"He is your friend, is he not?" asked the prince. The Sharshite only nodded. "And the Lady Fachalana is more than just a friend to thee, my lady," said Arsel, turning to Ansa.

"She is as my sister."

Oder might have smiled slightly at that.

"You watched me escort them into our home yesterday." Arsel seemed to look somewhere far away for a brief moment. "Yes, Fachalana entered our realm, but it is not for me to be her guide there, as I was for thee, Donzalo. Others have her care now." He gave Jobareth a nod. "And that of the loyal knight at her side."

"Then we must trust in your people to help her as they did me," said Donzalo. He looked about. "It seems we are heading back to Drolwym." Some on horseback, some afoot; they were not so very far from the haphazard keep of Thane Vantare.

"I shall remain a while. I sometimes come and sit here." The fay gave the graves another long look. "Fachalana is much like Jola and yet so very different. And both powerful enchantresses."

"I saw the sameness and the differences as well," admitted Donzalo. "Once I thought maybe the Lady Fachalana was my fate." He grinned at Ansa. "But I found otherwise."

Ansa was gazing elsewhere, to where a horse as gray as the mists of the Cuddon stood. "Jola's stallion," said Arsel. "He roams where he will across the hills but often visits here."

The horse came to Ansa and nuzzled her, as she stroked the sleek dappled neck. Then, satisfied, it turned and disappeared into those gray mists of the Cuddon.

~ ~ ~

"We are the folk some name Dark Elves," said the queen, "for we shun the bright light of the sun."

So had Sir Blen noted, in this dim-lit cavern the fay called their home. It was exceedingly large, the cavern, definitely too large to fit

7

into the hill where its gates lay. Someone might explain that to him someday.

"I had heard there were different, um, races of fay," he said, and immediately wished he hadn't. It sounded too stupid, too pointless. All he really cared about right now was Fachalana.

"Indeed there are. We are of many sorts in many worlds. Walk with me, child of the sun." She rose from her obsidian throne; the queen was as tall as Blen and her robe and hair were as white as her skin. Among the opalescent columns, arching into invisible heights, they passed. Among the folk of the fay they passed, some bowing, some oblivious, their minds elsewhere. All had the same snowy skin but hair color varied greatly. Perhaps some of those colors were not natural.

Likewise, clothing varied from the ornate to the nonexistent. Some—men and women alike—gave Blen looks of unmistakable interest. "You know of Jola?" she asked.

"Fachalana's sister. Half-sister. Daughter of Lord Radal. That's all." And that she had been involved with Sir Donzalo and the young Laman knight had been there at her death.

"Yes, Radal." The queen nodded solemnly. "We tried to shelter Fachalana from her father in his madness."

"Madness?"

"Radal was driven to madness. Oh, long had he teetered on the brink. That is a risk of human sorcerers and more so those of great power, who see further into the infinite worlds. Radal was the most powerful alive.

"But Jola. It was her death, the death of a daughter he did not know he had, that pushed him finally into the darkness. She too, came close to losing herself. She found herself when she dreamed here, after coming to us near broken. Now her sister must do the same."

"And she will be healed?"

"There is no way to know. She may die. Dreams can be perilous, Sir Blen, as we warned Donzalo. Yes, he dreamed here too, though his sickness was of a different sort. A sickness of the soul, not the mind."

"I—do not understand, your highness."

"That does not matter. I can tell thee Fachalana has come adrift among the infinite worlds. We must bring her back."

"When?"

"Tomorrow. The Lady Fachalana will sleep in the Chamber of Dreams tomorrow."

~ ~ ~

"The thane and his wife know me only as a bard and a friend of their son. Oh, I am sure they also knew I was his lover. But there is no need to say anything more." Oder sipped his wine, heated and spiced as Ani liked it, and propped his feet on the hearth.

"And they know I am your sister," Ansa reminded him. "It's too late to call that bird back to its cage."

"That might, ah, intrigue them a little but it is of no importance. I think they're more concerned as to whether you are worthy of our Donzalo."

"They are protective of him, aren't they? Maybe because he looks like another of Vantare's sons!"

"That he does. They're cousins but not particularly close ones." He gave his sister a bit of a wink and took another sip. "It does seem Jola's horse approved of you."

Ansa became pensive. "It has a bond of some sort with Donzalo. Perhaps only because he loved Jola. Fachalana's sister. I wish I might have known her." The young woman shrugged and brightened up, putting aside whatever mood possessed her for a moment. "Anyway,

I think its approval is worth more than that of all the Cuddonians put together!"

"If the two of you settle in these hills, you'll need their approval. You'll be Cuddonians yourselves. Hmm, that's something I need to discuss with Vantare." He sighed. "He may just have to learn I'm more than a mere minstrel."

"Don't disillusion him too much, brother mine. He loved his son and wouldn't like to think of him as but another of your tools."

"Guesare was more to me than that," Oder stated flatly. He was. He had loved the boy, in his way, and, moreover, considered him a friend. Oder was ever loyal to his friends. "What of you and the Lady Fachalana?" he asked. "Are you lovers?"

"You know that is not my way, Brother."

"I could never quite understand limiting oneself to lovers of only one gender."

Ansa gave him a look of exasperation. She had heard this before from her worldly sibling.

"Well," he said, perhaps a bit defensively, "it does all feel quite the same."

She had to laugh. "I would not know, Oder!"

"It's not that uncommon an attitude among professional soldiers," the Ani nobleman continued. "Lie with a whore one night, with a comrade in arms the next."

"And rape indiscriminately, as well. Boys, women—"

"Dogs, sheep," finished Oder. "I know, we are a most disreputable lot."

His sister's pensive expression had returned. "You are fortunate enough to have found a very different sort of man," he told her. "And a very good sort of man."

"Oh, that I know. I suppose the two of us will stay here through the winter."

10

"There are worse places to celebrate the Yule," said Oder. "And I am likely to be in one or another of them."

2

"Pirates, sir? Oh, aye, they are to be found in these waters."

Godos Tasetha looked out across the calm sunlit sea. From the corner of his eye, however, he could see the grins of the seamen. Were they baiting him? Best ignore it.

"More likely to meet smugglers, in truth, young sir," admitted one of the sailors. "These islands and secluded beaches suit their trade."

"And those of wreckers, too," another added.

"More of those further west," replied the first, a man as weathered as his ship. "When one reaches the Greater Sea and its storms, they can be a problem."

"But these islands might harbor pirates, mightn't they?" asked Godos. He was dreadfully bored and, moreover, fancied himself a fine swordsman. An encounter with pirates could break the monotony of this voyage.

It was a voyage approaching its end. If they hurried to port now, they might avoid those storms of the Greater Sea.

The young man, officially, was supercargo on this trading ship, a trim craft of three masts, two carrying sails of the triangular, Lorjam-rigged pattern. In truth, his family had bundled him off to sea to distance him from undesirable companions back in Celatas. Maybe he'll learn something of the business, his father had said. He hadn't sounded at all hopeful.

Around the isle of Lorj they had journeyed, stopping at ports both Partanacan and Coradean, and then northeast to Morparas, the Anian-controlled city at the mouth of the mighty River Weldar. Much of the wealth of Lama flowed through that city.

Some had flowed into their hold. They were homeward bound

with a cargo of this and that. Godos had been conscientious about keeping track of it. After all, what else did he have to fill his time?

Captain Ferstano emerged from his cabin. Until these last few days, none had bothered to sleep under cover. That was changing with the weather.

"The glass does not look good," the bearded sailor announced to any and all. He scanned the eastern horizon. "Nor does the sky."

"'Tis early for a winter storm," averred one the crew.

"Aye, and late for a hurricane, but both have been known this time of year."

Would they sail on? wondered Godos. Surely the captain wouldn't delay the return home, when they were so close. No good to say anything; Ferstano hardly paid attention to his existence, much less his opinions.

"We're still well east of Ussan and the Greater Sea. Best to pull into the lee of one island or another till the blow's over."

"The Landava is close, ain't it?" asked the first mate, who also happened to be Ferstano's mate. Seamen from Sharsh often took their wives along on their voyages. And sometimes women left their husbands home to mind the children and signed on as sailors.

"We should be closer to the Eph," felt her husband. "Neither river provides much of a sanctuary." His eyes went again to the east. "But I reckon we'd best find one somewhere."

~ ~ ~

"The wizard's body is on the way to Sharsh, my lady," reported Sir Jak. "I don't know why we couldn't bury him here."

"My father asked it," Lomela told him. For all his betrayal, Lord Radal had been the king's closest friend. "It is a small enough favor to keep Sharsh happy."

13

The burly knight nodded, remaining impassive. He had no love for the late sorcerer, the man he held responsible for the death of his master and friend—and Lomela's husband—the Count Bolos.

The man who was driven by his blind hatred of Donzalo Rosam.

"The ambassador saw the wagon off," Jak said, "and asked for a word with you. Shall I tell him to come in?"

"Certainly, certainly. Lord Doufan will always be welcome here."

Whether Jak thought that a good idea, the countess could not tell. But Doufan had proven himself a friend. That he would readily put that friendship aside if it interfered with his loyalty to Sharsh, she recognized. The man served her father, not her.

Doufan seemed particularly nondescript today. It was a manner the man cultivated, that of the suave, faceless courtier. Lomela knew him well enough not to be taken in. "My lady." He gave her a bow, just deep enough to be courteous without seeming obsequious.

"So Radal is on his way home?"

"He is. The body is to be interred at his country estate. That is what your father wishes. No ceremony."

"Quietly."

"That seems best, my lady. There is no reason to remind anyone of Radal and what came of him."

"Few loved the Lord Counselor." Lomela sighed. Another time, another place, she might not have allowed herself. "And many feared him. Yet I remember him as he was before he became our enemy, the father of my best friend."

"The Lady Fachalana."

"Yes." What had come of Fachalana? Had she arrived yet at the keep in the Cuddon? Found the healing they sought for her? "And what of you, Doufan? Will you be following Lord Radal to Sharsh? Ah, wine. Will you have some, my lord?"

A serving girl had brought a pitcher and goblets. Not Lomela's longtime maid, Dame Traspa. She had moved up in the world, wedding Sir Jak not so long ago. Doufan poured for both of them and followed the countess onto her small balcony, the only one in Castle Rosam.

"Lareth will send a new ambassador in time and I shall return to Celatas." Doufan chuckled. "Were Jobareth Nafal willing to remain in the king's service, it might not have been necessary to stay at all."

"I think perhaps you approved of his choice, sir?"

"I do. He will be more useful at your side than your father's. I am not sure whose side Sir Blen will choose." Both, undoubtedly, had ideas about that. "With your approval," the ambassador continued, "I shall carry Radal's effects back when I go."

"There wasn't much."

"Anything he carried on him was burnt in his final downfall. A few items survived in the lower rooms of the tower." Both turned their gaze toward the stone tower, the original heart of what grew into Keep Rosam. Its interior was being repaired even now, workmen coming and going. "A cask with a skull in it was the most notable of them."

"That might best have been destroyed too," Lomela felt. All of Radal should be swept away. He was the past.

"We shall permit the Lady Fachalana to decide that. The Viscountess Fachalana, I should say."

"Yes, Fachalana. I pray to Esefa that she will return to us soon, and as she was."

"I fear, my lady, she can never be as she once was."

~ ~ ~

Far to the south, another pair drank wine. "Were we in the open sea, I would not worry too much. It's a heavy blow but one we could

15

ride out. Amid these islands, it is another matter. Going aground is a danger." The door opened and closed quickly as the drenched first mate slipped into the cabin. "Ah, Wife. All well out there?"

"Pour some of that for me," said she, taking a stool. "The anchors are holding. When the wind shifts around we may need do something."

"The wind will change?" asked Godos. He hated to display his ignorance but he felt it was something he should know about. He might captain one of his father's ships himself someday.

"Aye," said Ferstano. "By the morrow it may well be blowing from the opposite way."

"But it's only a little blow," added the mate. She nodded toward the weather glass. "That trinket did prove useful."

Godos did not understand at all how the novelty worked, only that it was made from glass tubes blown in Celatas and it somehow forecast changes in the weather. He was truly more interested in the glass from which it was fashioned; Celatas had the best glass-makers in the world. He had a collection of their work back home.

Ah, home. He would be there soon! First, to the River Chas to unload their cargo at the great port of Azer, then up the river to the capital, Celatas. He should be able to make it in time for the Yule festivities. And the theaters would be open!

"I'll go up and look things over," decided Ferstano. "Come with me, young sir."

Godos rose, a bit unsteadily, to follow the captain. This pitching of the little ship was not good for the stomach. Undoubtedly, he should not have drank the wine, either, or at least not so much of it.

"Hang onto the line," ordered Ferstano, gripping a rope stretched fore and aft along the length of the deck. "Hmm, maybe we'd best get a rope around you too, boy. You look none too steady!"

16

He felt none too steady, and barely heard the man's words. His stomach was in upheaval. He was going to—

Godos reeled, retching, to the wooden railing and emptied himself into the sea. That was better, but he felt lightheaded as he rose from his crouch. Best he get back inside maybe. Yes, the dizziness was passing. Ferstano was holding out a hand to him, a grin on his face.

At that moment, a great wave rose to roll across the deck and Godos found himself in the turbulent waters of the Lesser Sea.

3

HE HAD REMAINED with Fachalana after the queen of the fay dismissed him. None said nay to this; indeed, little attention of any sort was being paid to Blen.

Fachalana was another matter. The elves were intrigued by this powerful sorceress, oblivious to them though she might be. They would come to the open doorway of the little room they shared, carved of the softly shimmering rock, and silently gaze at her, a minute or two before slipping away.

One, a woman, remained with them. How old? She appeared no more than a girl yet might have thousands of years of age. It would be best not to ask, though the knight doubted she would mind. She might not even know her age. The fay were not immortal; this he had been told by Jobareth, who had it of Donzalo. But they were immensely long-lived.

"It is good she eats," commented the elf-woman after a meal was brought and consumed. Blen thought it rather bland fare. Maybe the fay were just being careful with their guests, not knowing what they might prefer.

"Yes," he agreed. "She is as one in a dream, unspeaking, but seems aware enough to move about, to eat and to sleep. This is why we did not hurry too greatly in bringing her. There was—was hope she would return on her own."

A shaking of the head. "Not a good choice perhaps. But she is now here and we shall do what we can for Jola's sister."

In time, the queen came for them, accompanied by two male elves, garbed in dark tunics, swords at their sides and golden bands about their brows. They were the first weapons he had seen here. One was he who had greeted them at the doors of Faerie, the one who had named himself Arsel to Blen. Prince Arsel, the friend of Donzalo. Arsel, the long-ago lover of Jola.

"Come," spoke the queen. "It is time to find healing in dream." He followed down luminescent corridors, to halt before a tall silver door. "This is the Chamber of Dreams. It is the door to another world, even as is the gate through which you entered our caverns." She pulled forth an intricate key and opened the way.

Fachalana followed without urging, and Blen behind her. The two male fay remained without, taking positions on either side as the queen shut the door behind them. The size of the chamber was hard to determine, nor could one say exactly which way the white walls slanted.

"You may remain by Fachalana's side," she told Blen, "though you can not enter her dreams. Do not be alarmed by anything that happens, nor attempt to act, for there is naught you can do."

The fay took up a cup of what seemed sweet wine, spiced, by the scent of it. "Drink of this, and sleep," she told Fachalana. The young woman drained it without hesitation and reclined on a couch, as colorless as the rest of the room. Her dark hair spilled across it, standing in sharp relief.

Turning to Blen, the queen announced, "I myself will accompany her into another world. I do not need a draught for this."

So saying, she took a seat beside the noblewoman and closed her eyes.

~ ~ ~

"No, Jola had no children," Se told them. "But—" Her eyes went to her husband, who nodded his approval. "Our son had a child. Yes, despite his preferences, Guesare once let himself be seduced."

"*Let* himself?" asked Oder, an eyebrow raised.

19

"I've always suspected he was just curious," offered Thane Vantare.

"And curiosity sated, he never experimented again," said his wife. "That we know of."

"That is true," Se admitted. "Still, I doubt there were others."

"As would I," added the Ani.

"You just don't like him having had eyes for anyone else, brother mine," said Ansa. She sat close by Donzalo's side in this, the thane's private audience room. A variety of plain foods, including mutton prepared at least three different ways, covered the table around which they had gathered.

Oder came close to snickering. "The boy had eyes for just about everyone."

Vantare regarded his wife for a moment. "I've wondered if you pointed the girl at him. She is a member of your circle, after all."

"I might have encouraged her," she admitted. "Fausala has gifts and so will the child."

If any of this surprised the Anian spy-master, he didn't show it but sat sipping his beer. Donzalo suspected he already knew.

"Are any other of your grandchildren like Jola and, um—" No, he would not say that name.

But Se did. "Nosana? She did have a son. He might show powers some day or he might not."

"Nosana's child dwells with her late husband's people. Whether he was actually the father of the boy is anyone's guess," stated Vantare. "She neglected the child terribly. Even more so after her husband died."

After she murdered him, most believed. Donzalo had his own encounter with Nosana's potions and poisons.

"But none of the others," Se went on. "Or so it seems, though the heritage could certainly be there. Guesare would not have been a wizard were it not in his father."

"Nor Nosana," Jobareth reminded them. He had remained without words through most of this meeting.

"This is true," the priestess agreed. "Vantare's first wife had to carry the heritage as well."

"But it is another heritage we have met to discuss," spoke Oder.

"Yes, these two." Vantare squinted at Ansa and Donzalo, from beneath his shaggy white brows. "You are going to get married while you are here, aren't you? We can call the priest of Jov to make it official at any time."

"The Yule," I think, said his wife.

"Yes, splendid idea. You approve, Sir Oder?"

"I would prefer my sister wed in our homeland but I will not object." He might prefer she marry some Anian nobleman too. Donzalo did not care and was sure Ansa felt the same.

"Then the Yule it will be." That decided, the Thane stated, "None will prevent you from taking up residence in Sabatare's abandoned keep. That land has been wild and masterless for far too long. It seems the Ani approve." He nodded toward Oder, acknowledging he was more than a wandering minstrel. "We shall have to see about convincing the nobles to approve your title there."

"Title?" asked Donzalo. This had not been mentioned before.

"By rights, the name of Laird goes with the land. 'Tis hardly a title at all."

"Claim nothing higher," advised Oder.

"It is similar to a baronet in Sharsh, is it not?" asked Jobareth.

Oder answered. "Much like it, but a laird of the Cuddonian hills is likely to wield more actual power. There *will* be resistance among the clans to letting a Laman hold a keep in the Cuddon. Among my people, too. It will be seen as an encroachment from the valley—there is mistrust of Lama enough as it is."

"But Donzalo has Cuddonian blood, as do many nobles of Lama. My own family's blood," said the Thane.

"I am sure Sharsh will raise no objections," Jobareth said, and then gave a rueful smile. "Not that I can claim to speak for the king."

"Lareth would never even notice it were not Donzalo involved," Oder said. "So you, sir, shall speak to your fellow nobles and we shall see how it plays with them and I believe I need more beer."

As attentions returned to the meal, Ansa leaned close and whispered, "I'm not sure I want to wait until the Yule."

"Me neither," Donzalo agreed.

~ ~ ~

You may call me Munmirr, whispered the queen of the Fay. *We stand upon the Plain of Silver.*

I remember the plain, Fachalana murmured in reply. She was not certain she said it aloud. They were not exactly speaking from afar but something much like it. The fay at her side seemed more mist than substance. But the plain, the world, around her—that seemed solid. That seemed real.

An edifice of some sort over there. Almost at once, she found herself standing before its tall doors of silver. A temple–it seemed familiar. Hadn't she just passed through doors like those? It was so hard to remember, to be sure, as all the infinite worlds clamored in her ears, crowded into her consciousness.

Yes, she had once tried to hide behind those doors, hide from her father, certain her salvation lay on their other side. This woman at her side, she and her people, had attempted to help her.

This had been her place of peace. Fachalana had found it again. *If only I could remain here*, she whispered.

22

A part of thee can. I think a part of thee always has. That has kept thee from drifting away entire.

And I remember my way here now. I can always come. She turned toward her nebulous companion. *A little more solid now? Donzalo came here, didn't he? And my father came and tried to kill him.*

So I was told.

Yes, and I was with him. That is when I first learned of this Plain of Silver. She looked across the featureless expanse from her vantage on the temple steps, peered to where its horizons disappeared into silver mists. *I'm supposed to learn something here, aren't I?*

Perhaps. It is not for me to say.

My father. So many of his memories are within me. So much of him is with me since—since he fell. They were awakened and I have been fighting to keep them from taking me over.

But you see them now.

Yes. Yes. And I can place them where they belong and use them when I need. But I sense something more, some connection beyond that. Where? She sought. Beyond the silver light into the great darkness she sought, and suddenly gasped. *The realm of Asak. Part of my father yet remains there. It has been calling me all along, calling me to join it.*

To join Asak, not your father.

She recognized the truth of it. *Even so. What am I to do?*

Those who dream here seek answers. Perhaps there is one for thee.

Yes. Fachalana turned to the tall shining doors, flung them open.

There, above an alabaster altar, a halo of silver aglow about it, hung a great straight-edged sword.

The Sword of the Moon, whispered Munmirr, as Fachalana stepped forward to grasp its hilt.

She awoke in the Chamber of Dreams, a concerned Blen crouched at her side.

"You look terribly uncomfortable," she told him.

4

ALTHOUGH THE EMBASSY building was fairly complete, work continued on a courtyard area beside the stables. Those lay to the left as Lord Doufan rode up the low hill where the blocky limestone building perched. All the women here seemed to think it a very ugly building. The ambassador was inclined to agree.

Sir Blen had largely designed it, he was sure, though the legate, Jobareth Nafal, claimed equal responsibility. There was too much of the soldier about it. Doufan felt he might miss Blen's presence more than Nafal's.

But between King Lareth and the Viscountess Fachalana, it was unlikely he would be able to make any claims for the man's service. Yes, Fachalana. Others might not have recognized the growing bond between those two—perhaps not even Fachalana and Blen themselves—but Doufan had a lifetime's practice reading people. Blen, the quiet, the observant, the loyal. A man who would rather not be noticed, who had served for years as a royal courier in this land before catching Lareth's attention and being assigned as master of arms for the new embassy.

There would be no return to obscurity for Sir Blen. Blen Who? Doufan couldn't recall the man's family name, though it had appeared in various official papers. He dismounted in the courtyard, handed the reins to a waiting groom. This flat area had been dug out of the hillside, with a stone wall being laid about it and stairs at the rear to the second floor, where his own office and quarters were located.

For now, he would enter the embassy through the stables, rather than going around to the impressive front entry. Hardly anyone used that. Maybe it would all be finished before he returned to Sharsh. The young knight came from the lower Chas. He could have told that solely from his accent. But the ambassador had looked over what information there was on him before ever journeying here to take this post. Younger son of a small landholder, a baronet. He couldn't recall the name of the family estate either.

Ten years in the army, rising quickly to knighthood. Talented and smart, that was Blen. But not ambitious and perhaps a little too fond of routine. Also perhaps just the sort the Lady Fachalana needed. He would want to keep an eye on the both of them.

His scribe looked up as he entered his office but did not rise. "What's this?" Doufan asked, peering over his shoulder. "You don't need to practice your strokes after all these years, do you?" The man had filled a page with large, carefully penned letters.

"The legate asked me to write these for him. He says he'll carry them back to Celatas to show to a type cutter there." He looked up, giving his master the slightest of smiles. "He has friends with printing presses in the capital, and thinks they might be interested in my Lorjam style of lettering."

"Ah. Perhaps for his next book of poems. He has three out now, I believe."

"Even so, sir. They're not so bad."

Doufan laughed aloud, putting aside all his customary guardedness. He could do that with this man. "I shall take your word for it! All my favorite poets lived in the last century."

"Or that before it. Will you need me, sir?" The scribe looked approvingly at his last letter and put down his broad-nibbed pen.

"No, no. I need only a bath right now. Carry on—mustn't disappoint Lector Nafal."

But the nobleman wondered, as he passed up the hallway to his private chambers, if the young diplomat would ever find time to compose another poem. Lomela might keep him very busy in her service.

~ ~ ~

Where was the ship? He could see nothing in this darkness, with wave after wave towering over him. At least they were not breaking here. Godos turned about in a circle, treading water. No, the vessel seemed nowhere near.

There! A light, blinking and bobbing. That must be it. He stroked in its direction. Godos was a strong swimmer. His father had insisted he learn as a boy, at their summer retreat on the coast. Insisted? He had thrown him in and told him not to drown.

But the young man had come to enjoy swimming. He would have taken dips in the river back in Celatas had there not been so much sewage in it. Instead, he had found himself in the company of human sewage, those disreputable friends. Oh, yes, some of those were members of Prince Gawis's inner circle. Godos was on the outer edge of that circle himself.

Had been. Hand over hand. Was he getting closer? At least the water was warm, not at all like that in which he had learned to swim. The Greater Sea was chilly even in summer. The ship should stay in one place, shouldn't it? It was anchored. He would reach it.

Yes, the light was closer. One light, a lantern. Why was it so low to the water? Had Ferstano launched a boat to look for him? Ouch. Something had hit him. He reached out and grabbed at it.

"Hey!" someone cried out. "My oar is jammed on something."

"Help!" yelled Godos. "Help me!"

A few seconds later, hands were pulling him into a boat. "What in the name of Asak is anyone doing in the water here?" asked a gruff voice.

"I—I went overboard. My ship—somewhere."

"Toss him back?"

"Nah. He might be worth something."

The next thing Godos could recall was being wakened from a stupor by the grating of the boat's keel on a beach. A sheltered cove? He found himself sitting in the sand while the men—five of them—unloaded their boat. They were done by the time a gray dawn began to edge into the stormy skies.

The rain still came in sudden fits but it was not as it had been through the night. The boat could better be seen now. Not large at all, with a single mast. They wouldn't have been able to use a sail in last night's weather. What were they doing out in such weather anyway?

Smugglers, of course, just as the sailors had told him of. Coming over from Lorj, and they got caught by the same storm as his own ship. His father's ship. The captain probably thought him dead now and would sail away, carrying home the sad news.

Maybe he could get these men to go after the ship. He could offer plenty enough of a reward for it. One came over and gave him a long look. "Who be ye, boy?"

He rose, not as steadily as he might have wished. "Godos Tasetha. You would have heard of my family, sir."

The man spat on the sand. "Can't say what I have. Fell overboard in that bit o' weather, eh?"

"A wave carried me over."

A moment to consider that. "Ye probably know what sort we are."

"Traders, sir, the same as my own family, Just more, ah, secretive about it." He gave a weak smile and hoped the jest went over.

It did. In fact, the smuggler's guffaws lasted some time. "There would be gold in it if you could get me back to my ship," chanced Godos.

A firm shake of the dark, shaggy head. "We've our own business to tend. What have ye on yerself?" The fellow began to pat him down.

Not his sword. He had taken to no longer wearing that on deck after the first couple weeks of his voyage. It would have been hard to swim with it anyway. The man found his small wheel-lock pistol and then his dagger. Godos doubted he would ever see them again. "No cash? Nah, I guess ye wouldn't be carryin' that." He looked down at his bare feet. "And ye kicked off yer boots, I reckon."

"It was that or drown, sir." Though he had greatly regretted it. He had just purchased them new in Morparas, masterpieces of Laman leather work.

The other smugglers had joined them, ranging behind their chief.

"So what do we do with him?" came the question.

"Shoulda left him in the water," came one answer.

"We kin always throw 'im back," came another. "Or bury 'im right here."

Their leader shook his head. "Seems he's a gentleman. Might be worth a ransom."

"That can be risky." There was murmured agreement.

"Well, no matter, lads. We can decide after we finish doin' business. Galaro should be along soon."

~ ~ ~

"Do you think you might lose your position here?" Tiana asked her husband. It had been on her mind since things had settled down. Settled down some.

Sir Corgos could only shrug. He had not long been master of arms here at Keep Rosam before it was taken by Radal's henchmen. Some blame for that might be laid at his own feet. Maybe he should have been more vigilant.

STEPHEN BROOKE

Maybe he should have been more assertive, and spoken of his concerns to the late count Bolos. "There's much to do before the countess turns her mind to such questions, I think," he told her. "Sir Paren is in charge for now and is unlikely to make any decisions of that sort."

Paren, uncle of Bolos, was paying more attention to the rebuilding of the old stone tower. Its interior was damaged much by fire. The entire top floor needed replacement.

"And when Jobareth Nafal returns, he will be whispering in Lomela's ear," said Tiana.

"So it seems. Nafal is a good man. He has more brains that any of us, too. And—" He gave his wife a fond look. "I doubt anyone would throw us out when you are about to give birth."

No, but he might be moved to a different position, a lesser position, elsewhere. Then he and Tiana would have to give up their comfortable life at the castle. "When he returns, we shall have to confer on many matters."

"You and Nafal?"

"And Lady Lomela and Sir Paren and even Sir Jak, I would guess. We'll have to decide what to do with Jak."

"He won't take your job."

"That would seem unlikely." Jak didn't have the brains for it. His loyalty and honesty had made him well-suited to head Bolos's personal guard, but he couldn't run a castle. "I would be more concerned that Copago was called back. What is wrong?" His wife's face had contorted of a sudden.

"A contraction," she reported, and smiled. "They may have to evict three of us. Do fetch the midwife, will you?"

And Doctor Heragos too, Corgos told himself as he hurried down the hall.

5

"My brother is, in his way, quite the moralist. He is not cynical. Oder has a clear vision of his duty, not only to his people but to those who serve him. He does not use people and abandon them."

"But he has abandoned you," said Donzalo.

Ansa recognized her intended spoke this half-jestingly but chose to give a straight answer. "Only for a little while. He did promise to return for our wedding."

"I still think we're waiting too long."

"As do I. But I would like Oder to be there. And Fachalana *has* to be there. Of that there is no question." She looked at the very large young man she was to wed. "Impatient, are we?"

"How could I not be?"

"Oh, very good answer." She snuggled closer and considered using her lips for a kiss rather than to form words. "Oder wondered why we weren't already sharing a bed." At times, she did too.

"It is odd, isn't it? But we agreed to wait and perhaps we should stick with it." He sighed deeply and dramatically. "A whole month more!"

Yes, they had agreed. Before the doors of Drolwym they had agreed both to wed and to wait, and it was she who had added the second of those. It was the thought of Fachalana that led to her hesitation, that held her from giving herself to the man she loved. Everything could change. Everything remained in flux until they knew her friend was whole again.

"Ah, but you love me. You'll wait." This time she did give him a little peck on a cheek. She was glad he hadn't regrown the beard he reportedly sprouted when last he stayed in the Cuddon.

Donzalo had loved before. Jola. He had loved the lost Jola.

Perhaps he had loved Lomela, though she wasn't so sure of that. But he was the father of her son.

And now he loved her. Ansa had known lovers when younger, in her homeland, in the Anian Empire, but had never loved before. And she had eschewed any involvement during her career as a spy. All that was to change. Soon.

But here was this wonderful boy next to her right now. No, no, young lady, she told herself. Remember you pride yourself on your self-restraint!

"You know," she whispered, "if Fachalana came back soon we could move the wedding date up." Even if her brother would miss it.

"Maybe she'll want to get married too."

"Maybe." She gazed at the smoky peat fire for a few seconds. It didn't do much to keep this room warm. Thank—thank who? Thank some god or another for these good Cuddonian wool blankets.

She wasn't sure what gods she should be following now. Those of her homeland? The Kamat her husband supposedly reverenced? Or the old pantheon they worshiped here in the hills, not so unlike those of Sharsh. They were to be married by a priest of Jov, after all.

Fachalana. Might she marry Blen? She didn't truly know how things stood between them. The knight was devoted to her; that was obvious. But Fachalana had been difficult to read. Who could say how things would be once she was restored to them?

Ansa hoped her friend was being restored and said little prayers in her heart to gods of several different nations.

~ ~ ~

"She is not healed, but has only made a start at it," the queen told Blen.

Fachalana slumbered nearby. She had slept an inordinately long

31

time and the knight had begun to worry. Her snoring was also getting on his nerves.

"The Lady Fachalana has found the path she sought. We can take her no further nor need she again dream with us to follow it."

"But she will follow it."

"She must follow it."

"Ah." This was the sort of direct answer Blen preferred. Perhaps this fay recognized that. "And I shall support her in her journey as I can."

"I doubt it not. She awakens."

Fachalana sat up abruptly. "Where is my sword?"

"You can not bring that here from another world."

"Oh." Her consideration of the statement was quite brief. "Very well. Then where is something to eat? I am starved!"

"It is good to hear your voice again, my lady," spoke Blen.

"And food is on the way," Munmirr informed her.

"That's good. Oh, Blen, you have been watching over me all this time, haven't you? You and Ansa. I—I sensed you even if I didn't acknowledge you." Before the knight could answer she returned her attention to the elf. "I remember that sword coming to Donzalo from another world. It was the same sword, wasn't it? The one he used to battle Asak?" She paused, her brow furrowing as she seemed to strain to remember all that had happened in the chaos of that night. "Or to battle my father. Both, wasn't it?"

The queen nodded. "Asak had possessed Radal. But he did break free at the last. Part of him."

"Yes, part. I recognized that while I was on the plain. But what about the sword?"

Blen had to keep himself from smiling. This was the persistent and head-strong Fachalana he had come to love. Then he had to keep himself from weeping from the sudden rush of relief he felt. A great weight had been lifted from him, one he had not been willing to acknowledge all these weeks while he had remained at her side.

Two elves entered, bearing great platters heaped with cakes and jugs. He knew Fachalana might well eat them all; she'd had a rather prodigious appetite even at normal times.

"Donzalo wielded some aspect of the Sword of the Moon in that struggle. Perhaps even the one you grasped, the one behind the temple doors. We name that place the Temple of the Dawn."

Fachalana concentrated again, trying to remember. "I was really the one who held it, wasn't I? My sister—or was it Diba?—told me to seek it. Yes, I held the sword in two worlds at once, and its power flowed into Sir Donzalo and his own sword. Its *essence.*"

"Then it flew away from your world again when no longer needed."

"And I lost consciousness," Fachalana pointed out before popping a whole cake into her mouth.

"Indeed. But in an earlier battle, the one where your sister perished, he held another aspect of the sword, the one we guard here in our caverns. That you were able to find and to hold the Moon Sword in your dream, that it *chose* to reveal itself to thee, we take as a certain sign you are intended to carry it."

"For a time." Arsel stood in the doorway, holding a sword in a simple black scabbard.

"Yes, for a time," agreed the queen, rising. "Rest thee for a while, Lady Fachalana, and when you are ready, the prince will show thee the road to your friends."

"Good enough. We're in the Cuddon, right? I've always thought I'd like to visit." She drained her goblet. "I like this wine. What sort is it?"

"Mushroom," Arsel informed her. "And in the Cuddon we are,

my lady, or we will be when we step outside this realm of ours. They await you at Drolwym."

~ ~ ~

"It is a month and more yet to the Yule," Donzalo pointed out. "Are you certain you wish to stay? You have a wedding of your own to get back to, Habi."

The two were ensconced in the kitchens of Drolwym, enjoying the warmth of the cook fires and flagons of buttermilk. The brother of Habidros, Guesare, had introduced the young Laman to the drink. He was still not completely certain whether he liked it.

"As you, I came to see Lady Fachalana find healing. When she returns to us, I may think about going." He took a long pull on his drink. "Those sausages smell good, don't they? And someone's frying onions. We seem to get beef and nothing but beef at Tod-ford. 'Tis boring."

"But Lenasha isn't."

"Oh, no. She's a lovely lass and one I'm willing to finally settle down for. I've been a wandering mercenary far too much of my life, Donni."

That she was also niece to the lord of County Arvaram didn't hurt anything. "You two are suited to each other."

"That we are," the Cuddonian enthused. "I've never known a woman who rode so well!"

"Then you haven't seen my wife-to-be ride," Donzalo told him. "And don't think of trying to steal her, once you do."

"Oh, well, she's Anian. They're born in the saddle. Mighty uncomfortable for the mothers, I must say."

Donzalo smiled, though he'd heard the joke before. More than once.

34

"Also," Habidros went on, "she's mighty small. Lenasha is more my size. Or your size, for that matter."

He did tower over Ansa, though she wasn't really that small. Donzalo was simply tall. As was the man across the table from him. "We're going to get bored," he said. "You sooner than me, I suspect."

"Aye, with my brothers gone back to their farms and your friend Oder off to who-knows-where, it's slow in Drolwym. Nafal just sits and writes and daydreams. Does he have a woman to get back to too?"

"I think his daydreams are of the Countess Lomela."

"Oh! I should've seen that before because I can certainly see it now." He gave Donzalo a long moment of scrutiny. "That doesn't bother you any, does it?"

"Not at all. Bolos is gone and I think they both care for the other." To be sure, his relationship with Lomela, the Sharshite princess who had married his brother, was decidedly complicated. None of that would Habi know, nor should he. "What do you say we ride? I might even be able to get Ansa to come along."

Half an hour later, the three were galloping across the rounded, heather-covered hills. Brown and gray; those were the colors of the Cuddon, at least on this day. This season.

"Those standing stones are where Se and her priestesses meet," Donzalo announced, pointing to the hilltop shrine of Rema.

"Naked," added Habidros. "Even in this weather. My mom's tough." He seemed the only one of Se's stepsons who wholeheartedly accepted her as his mother. Guesare had once hinted a teen Habi had a crush on her.

"And up ahead is the shrine of Diba."

"Oh, Diba the Huntress?" asked Ansa, reining in her shaggy pony. "I remember you mistaking me for the goddess once, Donni. Can we go inside?"

Habidros gave him another of those long looks. "Are you comfortable with it? I know this place has memories for you. Guesare told me of your vigil here."

Ansa had alit. "Vigil?"

"In preparation for being named a knight. The thane dubbed me the next morning. The Yule, it was."

"But it was more than an ordinary vigil. More of an ordeal from what I heard," said Habidros. "Set upon by demons and witches and phantoms!"

Donzalo had to laugh. Yet it was true; it was also the beginning of the road that led to Jola, to her love, to her death. "Your sister Nosana did try to give me some trouble," he said. And not the first time.

Curiosity satisfied—there was little to see in the small shrine, a single room with a statue of the goddess—Ansa remounted and they rode on. The skies were low and sullen. Crows glided silently above the hill crests. Before them lay a taller hill and, nestled below it, a grove of pines.

Ansa would recognize this place. She had been here when they laid Guesare to rest. "I would like to visit for a minute or two," he said, to either or both or maybe just to himself, and rode slowly down toward the cottage, the graves, the memories of the great love and the great tragedy of his young life.

He was sure Ansa understood. She knew he loved her none the less.

Of a sudden, she let out a whoop and spurred her pony past him, careening down the hill!

6

"HERE THEY BE at last," growled the leader. The other smugglers looked up from the little fire around which they huddled. The wind had died enough to permit it and there was a new nip to the air this evening.

All day they had waited. Godos, they ignored. He was exceedingly hungry.

A larger man—no, a huge man—strode into the makeshift camp, half a dozen rough-looking fellows behind him. Mostly fellows. That one was a woman, wasn't she? She looked rather rough too.

But none unkempt and slouching like these smugglers. Their leader's eyes flicked toward Godos but he ignored his presence through the rest of the meeting. There was haggling, there were complaints, there were coins paid, and the newcomers began carrying away the goods the smugglers had brought ashore.

Another time, Godos might have been interested in knowing what those goods were. Now, he was too miserable and too fearful to care. "Who's the kid?" asked the giant.

"We found him floating in the drink. Went overboard sometime during the storm."

"We're thinking he's worth a ransom," added one of the men.

"Might be more trouble than it's worth," said the big man. He was nearly a head taller than the chief smuggler, and broad, with a great black beard.

"Aye. That be so," the smuggler admitted.

"Maybe I could manage it. I'll tell you, I'll take him off your hands and give you, mmm, three Royals in the bargain."

"Five," the smuggler countered at once.

"Four and no more. Done? Good enough. Come along, lad."

A minute late, Godos was marching with this new group of

companions. "I would never have left you with that trash, boy. They would have decided you were too much bother and slit your throat after a while." He looked over his men. "And they knew I had the upper hand if they weren't willing to make a sensible deal."

"So—so what will you do with me, sir?"

"Call me Galaro. What's your name?"

"Godos, sir. Godos Tasetha."

"Tasetha? As the Tasetha fleet?"

"Fronos Tasetha is my father."

Galaro threw back his head and laughed uproariously. "They really could have made good money off you! I only trust you to get me back my five Royals one of these days."

"Four, sir."

"Yes, a Tasetha indeed."

~ ~ ~

"He's not a very talkative little lad," Dame Traspa told her husband. "Not for his age. But I don't think he's at all slow."

"So was his Uncle Donzalo. Barely said a word till he was four or so. But active! We were forever chasing after the scamp. Eager to explore every corner of this keep, he was." Jak momentarily sobered. "Bolos was a quite different sort of boy."

"He could be, um—" Traspa searched for a proper word, one that did not imply any judgment of the late count. "Indolent." Yes, that was a fine word, one a lady might use. Traspa had spent her adult life, and much of her childhood, serving ladies.

"Lazy, you mean. That he could. But he wanted to be the man he should, when he wasn't in his cups." Jak stared into space for a little while, absently stroking his beard. "I think he managed it in his final days."

Lomela's former maid believed it too. Best maybe to change the subject. It didn't do for Jak to be brooding over the past. "The cottage was nice enough but I missed my friends here. It's good to be back in the keep," she said. "With something to do."

"You mean you missed gossiping. But aye, it is good to have duties again" agreed the knight, and then chuckled. "Now I'll be busy chasing after little Ros."

"Both of us." As she had chased after little Lomela back in Sharsh. They had come full circle, now charged with doing for the child what once they had done for the parents. Jak was to be Ros's personal guard, as he was his supposed father's. Traspa was one of the very few in on the secret that Donzalo was truly the boy's father.

Her unquestioning loyalty to her Lomela kept that secret safe. Not that it would matter much now, would it? Young Ros would be count either way, though Donzalo could wear the title first. She knew he did not want it.

And another was in her mistress' heart now. If King Lareth had consulted her she would have told him years ago to marry the girl to Jobareth Nafal, not some distant Laman nobleman! But then—she gave her husband a long, fond look. He wasn't handsome, stout and bald, but she loved him with all her being.

"What is it, woman?" came his good-natured query.

"I was only thinking how had things gone a bit differently, we might never have met."

"Destiny is not just for our betters," said Jak, kissing his wife.

~ ~ ~

"These are the wildest, most dangerous lands of any through which we travel," Galaro was telling him. "The Coradeans supposedly control the coasts and Count Orgelo holds sway further north, but here it is lawless."

Wherever 'here' is, thought Godos. The traders' caravan had

traveled north, mostly, from the coast. He was sure it was north. The skies had cleared and one could now track the sun's passage across them. Seven they were, leading a string of pack horses laden with whatever goods they had received from the smugglers.

Into ever-rising terrain they led them, from rolling, sandy, scrub-covered land into pine-clad hills. "That mount was intended to carry goods, not humans," Galaro continued, as they rode along. "Better than walking though, eh?"

"That it is, sir." He sensed it unwise to question this man too closely, but did venture, "Are we near Pas?" The largest port along these coasts. He could find passage to Sharsh from there.

"Pas is well west of us. We're crossing into the valley of the Eph."

Galaro let him digest this information before going on. "The rest of my troop waits there. Some of them; those that have homes and families oft spend the winters with them."

"Sir—" He hesitated.

"Spit out whatever it is you want to ask."

"Not to be too forward, but what are you? I mean, where are you from? I've never heard an accent like yours." And Godos had heard a great many different accents. That was unavoidable in his father's house.

A deep, rumbling chuckle. "I'm from the Cuddon. A good place to be from but not so good a place to stay."

Wild Cuddonians were a staple caricature of the stage in Celatas. Bearded and kilted and none too bright, usually. Godos had sense enough not to mention any of that, but this Galaro did look the part!

They stopped in late afternoon when their track crossed a wide, dirt roadway. Galaro gestured both directions, saying, "This is the main road running west from Ephnas to Pas and to Arlacas beyond. We will not travel it but cross it as quickly and as unobtrusively as we can."

Godos nodded. He understood the reasons. Understood them enough.

"If you want we can set you down here. It's not too long a walk down to Ephnas and you might find a ship there to carry you home. But you'll need to pull your weight if you travel on with us."

The young Sharshite looked down the road. There was no guarantee of any welcome in Ephnas and he was without money. Perhaps an adventure awaited if he crossed this road. Perhaps he could put off a return to the boring life his father had planned for him back home.

"I'll try sir," he said.

"You'd best do more than try. And call me Captain now you're one of us." Galaro shook his reins and led his little band across the road.

7

WHERE THE ELVES kept their horses Fachalana had no idea, but three saddled mounts waited for them as they passed the doorway. Blen turned and looked back when they were outside, shaking his head. "I can't see it at all from this side, but I know it's there."

Fachalana looked too. The opening to the realm of the Dark Elves was quite obvious to her. But—it wasn't really in this world, was it? It was like those other worlds she and all sorcerers could see. Different though. No time to think about that now. She mounted and followed Arsel. Northward, through a dark, scented, pine forest they rode.

There was a path, narrow but obviously used from time to time. "Do your people travel here?" asked Blen. "Or is this but a trail made by animals?"

"It is a path I have made myself over many years. I often travel this way."

"Toward Drolwym," murmured Fachalana. "Toward Jola."

"Yes," answered the fay, and no more.

They emerged from the wood by a little sod-roofed cottage. She knew at once what cottage it was. There was no need to say anything.

But someone was certainly hollering! A rider came charging down the slope toward them. "Halloooo! Faaachalaaaana!"

"I believe that is Ansa," remarked Blen, but Fachalana was already spurring toward her friend.

Both women reined in their steeds and sat regarding each other for a few seconds. "So, Lady Fachalana, you have decided to return to us?" asked Ansa.

"It seemed the thing to do." Then both were on the ground and embracing.

Ansa stepped back, holding her friend at arms' length. "Oh, Fachalana, I feared so for you. Have you truly returned? Are you whole again?"

"Wholer," laughed the noblewoman, and then gave it a moment's thought. "Maybe wholer than ever I have been in my life." But there was more to be done, much more. There was no reason to say anything of that.

The others had gathered around them now, greeting her and Blen as if they had been years apart. Fachalana was sure it was but a few days; it was impossible to note the passage of day and night in the caverns of the fay and she had been in a timeless fog before that. She looked about. "It's autumn, right?"

It was Donzalo who laughed. "A month to the Yule." Then his eyes went to the sword at her side. "I recognize that blade. It is the one I once wielded."

Habidros nodded. "They would know it well at Drolwym. I saw it when Mausare had its keeping."

"Yes, for Jola, before he passed it to me." His attention returned to Fachalana. "The Fay told me the Sword of the Moon would remain with them until it was again needed."

"It seems it is," spoke up Arsel. "We know not why but it chose to go with Fachalana."

"I'm almost afraid to use it," Fachalana admitted. "It would be good to have a sword in my hand again. I could go back to soundly out-fencing our good Sir Blen."

"Any day, my lady," said Blen, giving her a bow. "You might find Donzalo a more challenging opponent; he too has shown he quite outclasses me."

"Even Guesare felt his large student here was one of the best he'd known. Maybe even better than he himself was, and that is saying more than a bit," added Habidros.

"Well, then we must cross swords, sir. And who is this?" A tall stallion, all dappled of gray, had quietly joined them.

"Jola's horse," whispered Ansa. "He was friendly to me but I doubt he would ever have let me ride him."

"None but Jola have ever ridden him," Arsel told them.

Fachalana reached out, stroking the steed's back. "You would let me ride, wouldn't you?"

As if in invitation, it turned its side to her. She did not think of hesitating but pulled herself up. A shorter woman might have found that more difficult. Bareback, astraddle, her bare legs sticking out of her gown, she sat and looked down at her companions, smiling broadly.

She heard Donzalo's quick intake of breath and knew at once she reminded him of her sister. "He tolerates me," she announced, "but I do not think he would ever permit himself to be saddled."

"I agree, my lady," said Arsel. "Nor do I know if he would be willing to be with thee beyond these hills. He is linked to them as he was to your sister."

She caressed the stallion's neck. "And he sees her in me. No, you'll never be my horse, will you? But we can be friends."

"Sometimes I think, too, he has some link to the Plain of Silver. That is beyond what I can see, or any of my people." Arsel bowed to her and turned to the rest of the company. "And now I return to those people." Without further word, he mounted and rode back the way they had come, leading the horses she and Blen had ridden.

"So, who's going to give our poor horseless Blen a ride?" asked Fachalana. "I want to see this keep and have a good meal and a good sleep!"

"Behind me," said Habidros and five rode to Drolwym on four horses.

44

~ ~ ~

"Then you will become a priest this coming summer?"

"I will, my lady. At last." The events of the year now nearing its end had postponed Brother Grippo's entry into the priesthood of Kamat. They had nearly convinced him not to take orders at all.

"Jobareth will not like losing his secretary." Lomela did not seem to think that a serious concern. "Though there is a perfectly good scribe who served Count Borrago and continues in our service."

"Madin. A good man and a discreet one."

"And of course you will continue to have access to the castle and our friendship."

"My superiors permitting, my lady."

"Oh, you know the hierophant will do pretty much what we ask of him. Ha, even if we don't ask, we'll probably always be suspected of favoritism toward you."

The countess was astute. "It is something I shall have to endure," said Grippo, grinning.

"Yes, poor Grippo. It's cool out here." With that, she turned and went back inside her chambers. Grippo followed, taking care to securely close the door to the balcony behind him. With little Ros running about, one had to be careful.

He napped in his nursery at the moment. "I finally received a message from the Cuddon," spoke Lomela. "They all arrived at this keep to which they were heading and where the Lady Fachalana is supposed to be healed. There was little more to it."

"I have prayed to Kamat for her healing."

"And I to Esefa. Do you think it does any good?"

"We know Asak harmed her. Who better than his eternal adversary Kamat to heal her?" He couldn't resist adding a lopsided smile to this. Grippo had a sense of humor and did not take his pronounce-ments overly seriously.

"You'll never make hierophant if you can't maintain a grave manner," the countess told him. "And we have such hopes for you."

"More than I do, I am sure." This he would miss, this banter, when he went to live among the other priests. He would miss the sophistication of Lomela, of Jobareth Nafal. Of Lord Doufan, for that matter. The ambassador would be leaving soon, it was said.

And Donzalo would never return. Not as a resident.

"What wool are you gathering, Grippo?" asked the countess.

"Thinking of all my friends, my lady, and how I will miss them. How I miss some of them now."

She only nodded to this. She surely understood. "Read to me, will you?"

"Some of those lurid tales Countess Vibola loved?" he asked. The old woman had indeed been fond of them. Lomela had sometimes read them to her herself.

"No." She went to a shelf and retrieved a slim volume. "Here. Jobareth's latest collection. Give me something from it."

He leafed through the book. "Here's one," he decided. 'Bow.'"

Lomela reclined in a chair upholstered in green velvet, waiting for him to begin.

What bow has set me to this futile flight,
Has sent me arcing to your armored heart?
Dare I trace the journey of that dart
To some willful archer of the night,

Some jokester god who, laughing, took his aim
At a mark no man might penetrate,
Leaving me to curse both love and fate?
No, I will myself take all the blame

And know I was a fool, as are men all,
For we choose to fly and, spent, must fall.

Neither spoke for a little while. "I didn't realize it for a long time," said Lomela at last, "but that poem was addressed to me. Don't you think so, Brother Grippo?"

"I do, my lady."

"Yes, far away in Celatas he was remembering me and putting on paper what he dared not say to a princess, much less a married one. Do you think, Grippo, we could marry?"

"Not at once maybe," he said. "It wouldn't look right. And—" A broad grin once again stole onto his face. "You must wait until I am a priest so I can perform the ceremony."

"We would have it no other way."

~ ~ ~

"You're not my bodyguard anymore, Habi. You don't need to stay."

"But I'd miss the wedding."

"Better than missing your own. Get yourself south while the weather is still not too bad and get Jobareth south with you. He's the one who needs a bodyguard."

Habidros drained his cup. "Very well. But we must throw a bach-elor party for you before we leave."

Donzalo groaned, inwardly. He had hoped that custom would be forgotten. Why, it wasn't even a Cuddonian tradition, but a Laman one. "Let us call it a farewell banquet instead," he suggested. That sort of thing very much was a Cuddonian tradition.

"Is Nafal prepared to return?"

"He is. He knows it's best to go before winter sets in, too. I suspect Ansa and I shall be here till spring."

"And Lady Fachalana."

"Yes. It is for her we remain. She still needs to rest. To heal." That took time. He knew that as well as any and better than most. "And, of course, Blen will stay where she stays and go where she goes. Even if King Lareth himself called for him."

"I wonder," said Habidros, "if she would do the same for him."

"Let us hope," came Donzalo's reply, "that Blen never needs to find out."

"I'll drink to that. There is more beer, isn't there?"

"Ale. It's ale and there is a keg over there. Freshly brewed though it's cool enough to make beer now."

"As you say. I just drink it and don't worry how it's made." The Cuddonian refilled his cup and returned. "Ah, but you like to know how things work. Like with your making of gunpowder. Will you be getting back to that?"

"It's possible. That keep where we're looking to settle could be a good spot for it. I could get sulfur from the lower Siph instead of the far side of Lama or even farther Ussan."

"And sell it to the Ani?"

Donzalo could only shrug. He would be an Anian subject, with an Anian wife whose brother was high in the imperial councils. Why not deal with the Ani?

"You'd do better to make beer," felt Habi. "Or even ale."

"Maybe so. I'd like seeing where it's brewed here. Do you know if there's a malting floor somewhere about the place?"

"I don't even know what one is," answered Habridros. "But I'm sure you will tell me."

"Some other time. Let's get back to your departure. The sooner you go, the better, you know. You might even make it back to Tod-ford for the Yule if you left right now."

"Hmm." Habidros was probably thinking of the distances involved. "I doubt it. But we could get Nafal to Ros-town by then. I wouldn't mind spending the Yule there."

Neither would I, admitted Donzalo Rosam, only to himself.

8

A RAGGED MUSKET volley opened the attack. Not one man nor woman fell but a stricken horse reared and then went down. The bandits broke from cover, charging the caravan with a motley assortment of spears, swords, and pole arms.

Godos had no weapon other than the knife Galaro had lent him, better for peeling vegetables than fighting. Indeed, peeling vegetables had been among his chores; as newest member of the troop his were the most menial of tasks.

He had no time to think of any of that right now as a dark man in a jack-coat thrust a sword toward him. Godos at once slipped off the other side of his horse and emerged from behind it, knife in hand. His opponent only laughed when he spied the puny blade—laughed until the young man easily slipped past his guard and plunged it into his chest.

The other bandits had fared no better. Already they were bolting back into the brush, recognizing they had attacked the wrong sort of travelers. These were fighting men—yes, and women—as well as traders.

Galaro strode over and gave the dead man a cursory glance. "So knife-fighting is among your skills."

It was. "My fencing master in Celatas insisted his students learn to use all blades, not only the sword." This was not to say he had ever before wielded a knife in a real fight.

And he had certainly never killed anyone.

"Then you can handle a sword." The big Cuddonian waved an arm toward the corpses the traders were already stripping and placing in a pile. "It seems we have a few spares now. Choose one for yourself." He then glanced at the boy's bare feet. "Maybe you can find a pair of boots to fit you too."

Perhaps some did but Godos hadn't the stomach for stripping off a pair. Nor did they look to be in very good shape, even the best of them. He did find a decent enough sword and none prevented his appropriating it.

Half an hour later they were again on their way, shorter by one horse. Godos had to take some of the load it carried behind him. A crate dug into his back, making for a less than comfortable ride. "We've not lost much time," Galaro told him. "This is part of the cost of doing business in these parts."

"Are bandits common, sir, er, Captain?"

"Scum such as these, southerners for the most part, hang about the port towns looking for opportunities. Sometimes banditry, sometimes piracy. Wreckers too—" He paused a moment and frowned. "I'll admit I've done business with wreckers, despite finding it distasteful."

"A profit is never distasteful," ventured Godos.

"Ha, again, verily a Tasetha. And here is the River Eph. We'll be crossing it up here and soon be with the rest of my crew."

Godos wondered just how many that might be. He would find out, wouldn't he? The horses waded the shallow, rapid stream, and they rode on.

~ ~ ~

She could find the Plain of Silver as quickly as a thought now. Nothing happened there but it was place of peace, a place where she could rest, a place where the voices of the infinite worlds were muted.

But Drolwym was also a place to rest. She had met Lady Se there, the mother of her half-sister—a woman her father had loved when he passed through here when young and in exile from Sharsh. How might Radal's life have been different had he put aside ambition and remained here with her?

Ah, but then there would be no Fachalana. That would be no good! She peered into the silver haze concealing the plain's horizons. Did anything exist beyond them? Was this the totality of this world?

That world faded and she returned to her cozy room. It was shared with Ansa, at the request of both women. Unlike some, Fachalana was not at all surprised Ansa had held off on sharing a bed with her husband-to-be. She certainly didn't intend to do anything of that sort before she wed.

She would wed, wouldn't she? Wed Blen. Not that he had asked her. She might have to propose herself! Not yet. Not until she was more sure of herself. Blen probably recognized that too. That was why he had said nothing.

Or did he still feel his station was not high enough? He might have become close to powerful men, to Lord Doufan, even to the king himself, but he was still but an ordinary and near-penniless knight. And she was Lady Fachalana, Viscountess Ildoram, and apparently quite wealthy. She had never needed to think about money before.

Fachalana loved Blen. That she knew, even though she had never loved any man before. Yes, there had been an infatuation with Donzalo, mostly with his reputation. That had faded some as they got to know each other in person.

Donzalo had his destiny and it was not her own destiny. Give her time and she might just figure out what that was.

~ ~ ~

There were wagons and at least a dozen more men and women in Galaro's camp. Godos was a little surprised to learn the big Cuddonian did not hold unquestioned authority here.

"We are free traders," one woman told him. "Galaro we elected captain and we are satisfied with the job he does, but we could elect another were we not."

"And all the big decisions are voted on," said another trader. Godos only nodded and peeled another turnip.

They held a council that night for that very purpose. "I say we strike north for one last time this season, before it gets too cold," proposed Galaro.

"How far north?" came a voice.

"County Rosam at most. Maybe not that far. Then find our way back down the Weldar and trade across the south."

"Better 'n sitting here doing nothing," opined a one-eyed man. He had been pointed out to Godos as Galaro's second so it was to be expected he would support his proposition.

"But would we make a profit?" asked another.

"We won't sitting here, that's for sure," someone replied.

"We've barely more than half our strength."

"But enough," spoke Galaro. "It's not like we're going to the great Summer Fair."

And so it went but in the end every voice said *aye* to trading north.

Of course, Godos and various other hirelings had no voice in the decision. "It's rare we do much business this time of year," Galaro told him later. He sometimes wondered why the burly trader chose to converse with him. It just might have something to do with his family, though he preferred to think he was simply an interesting young fellow. "Spring's the season for it but I'd rather not sit on our goods till then."

"Is it safe to travel?"

"We could still run into more bandits. They'd be less likely to attack a troop this size. Southern Lama is safer than these parts, too, though no place is without its dangers."

Godos took this in. "Then I'd like to stick with you, if you're willing. Um, do you think maybe I could send word to my parents?"

Galaro gave an amiable nod to this. "That could be done readily enough further north. Your name would be sufficient to get one more letter tucked into a courier pouch." He cocked his head at the boy. "I thought you weren't in a hurry to get back, lad."

"No, Captain, but I'd rather not have them think me dead." Godos couldn't help grinning as he added, "And as long as I'm in Lama they can't marry me to anyone."

"You might be surprised at how many have similar reasons for being here."

9

"Not so long ago, we led Donzalo this way," said Habidros.

Jobareth knew that tale. "And you're sure it's the quicker route?"

"For two men on horseback, yes. Well, probably." The Cuddonian flashed a grin. "That depends on how quickly you're willing to ride."

More on the horses than the men, suspected Jobareth. Each led a second mount so they might change frequently, or in case one came to harm.

They had wound through the hills of the Cuddon to reach this little dirt road, rutted by wagon wheels, leading westward. It would connect with the Great Road somewhere ahead, and they could turn south, paralleling the Weldar. One could make good speed on the paves of the Great Road—and Jobareth still carried Sharshite diplomatic credentials to get him quickly across any borders.

How many borders lay between them and County Rosam he was not sure. There was a patchwork of little counties up here, in the lands south of the city-state of Oles. Fortunately, they would miss that municipality. Nafal had visited it with Lord Doufan, and thought it thoroughly hideous and its citizens repellent. From there, their party had taken boat down the Weldar to Ros-town.

That was not an option for this journey. They were descending a steep grade. "And there's the road," announced Habidros. "See the river beyond? It's a grand view."

"Not as grand as Castle Rosam rising on its cliffs," he replied. "The sooner I can see that, the better."

"Ah, Lector Nafal, for a poet you seriously lack an eye for beauty. Let's ride."

~ ~ ~

Dorbi's Crossing they had named the inn. Though Perdos had been at its repair since they arrived—even before they officially owned the place—there was still much to do. But it was ready enough for him and Rassana to do business, to open the doors to guests.

Rassana—at times he still couldn't believe the woman was with him. Married to him, too. She had insisted and he was willing enough.

It didn't matter that he had used a false name, did it? Or was it truly false? He was Dorbi now. Perdos he had left behind; he was no longer that disreputable knight, a man who had done both evil and good, but had to make way for Dorbi the innkeeper. Dorbi his wife had named him, claiming she had called a favorite dog of her youth so. He was willing enough to accept that too.

"It's too bad there aren't any chestnuts around here," said Rassana, busy with something in the kitchen.

Dorbi-Perdos agreed. "I remember them back home. They were always a part of the Yule." The woman and he had grown up not so far from each other in the upper reaches of River Weldar but had never met until the day he stopped by her food stall in Ros-town.

He was not certain yet whether she or her food was the more irresistible. No matter—they came as a package.

Not that his wife would do all the cooking here. Dorbi knew his way around a kitchen and he had taken on Hendel, the disgraced pastry cook of Castle Rosam, to help out. A minor partner, in fact, Hendel would be. The man had put up a little booth down by the ferry landing after the owners here had been murdered and the place burnt. It had not been hard to convince him to throw in his lot with the couple.

Ah, those innkeepers. He had avenged their deaths as Perdos, and that was good. They had treated him well when he spent a winter— last winter, it was—here and even suggested he invest in the place. He did recognize his horse-thieving and killings had led at least in part to their deaths and felt some regrets. But no guilt. He had done the things he had to do.

A pair of ferry guards sauntered in. It must be the changing of their shift. "Ale, gentlemen?" asked Dorbi. Dorbi, the proprietor of *Dorbi's Crossing*.

~ ~ ~

There could well have been an arranged marriage awaiting Godos when he returned from his voyage. His parents had made more than a few suggestions as to women he might marry but had so far not insisted on one. They argued now and then as to whether an alliance with another powerful merchant family or some minor noble house might be more advantageous. Mother and father would probably agree to any decent match now—or would when they learned he was alive. They might begin plotting at once.

It was fortunate he was a younger son. They had demanded much more of his brother.

Galaro demanded hard work. There was much loading of pack horses and mules, and of great wains. Everything must be in just the right place so it could be easily produced for sale as they reached each marketplace. Godos was assured there would be much loading and unloading in his near future.

But all these traders took part in it. There were no shirkers amid the troop of Galaro. The captain had seemed amused when he told him he had been supercargo on a vessel and knew about keeping track of goods. "If you can keep the list in your head, that's fine, lad. We write nothing down here."

On thinking about it, that seemed logical with smuggled goods. No written records, no taxes levied! But he didn't think he could ever keep track of everything. No need, anyway; he wouldn't be here all that long, he told himself, as he helped hoist another crate into another wagon.

Then they were rolling, rolling northeastward into more rugged country, climbing out of the valley of the Eph. Out of the lands claimed by An Corade and into Lama proper.

~ ~ ~

"Sir Blen."

The knight turned to see Prince Arsel of the fay, not that he hadn't recognized the voice. The fay simply sounded different from mortals, though he couldn't put a finger on what exactly that difference was. There was a certain lilt to his speech.

"Arsel. I greet you."

"And I thee." The elf gave him a friendly smile. "You wander?"

Blen smiled in return. "I can only sit in Keep Drolwym for so long."

"I understand. It is why I wander myself; I find life in our caverns more wearying than most." Both wandered a little way across the heather, side by side. The sun was hidden, as usual, but the day was not so dreary as some. Blen could see a beauty in it.

"You spend your lives there?"

"Oh, no. There are other gates than the one you and Fachalana passed. Gates to many worlds, if we wish to explore them." He gazed at the hills about them. "I have been content with this one for some time."

"And I must be!" Blen answered, with a bit of a chuckle.

"If you wish to remain with Fachalana, yes, though men too can pass the gates into uncounted other worlds. Fachalana sees those worlds, visits those worlds, without using gates, as do all those with the power of sorcery."

"Then I had best be here when she gets back."

58

"Even so. You will be the anchor that keeps her from drifting." Perhaps he smiled again at the knight's expression. "So we believe."

Arsel did not follow that with any explanation but changed the direction of their conversation. "We have been visited by a goddess. Not in person, but she spoke in our queen's dreams."

Blen could think of many goddesses, some of his homeland, some of elsewhere. "Should I know of this goddess?"

"We believe this as well. She is Diba."

Diba the Huntress was barely remembered in Sharsh, but lived in the folk traditions of Lama, where they did not follow her pantheon at all. There was a temple to her here, wasn't there? She must be more important in the Cuddon. "Does she have something to do with the Lady Fachalana?"

Arsel seemed uncertain. "She was friendly to Jola. A patroness, one might say. And she aided Donzalo and even seems to have some connection to his beloved. Fachalana? We can not guess what interest the goddess has in her. But," the fay went on, "she spoke of another sword. And she spoke of thee, Blen of Sharsh."

A sword? Blen was no one to be mentioned by goddesses or to be involved with mystic swords. Leave such things to others—he was but an ordinary knight.

"She said only that you would find a sword. No, that is wrong. Diba said you should seek a sword. Nothing beyond that."

"Then I suppose all I can do is keep my eyes open."

"So it would seem, Sir Blen. That and do all you can to help Fachalana in the trials to come."

10

"WHAT ARE WE to do about the secret passage?" asked Sir Corgos. "It is not so secret anymore."

"Rumors of it are common down in the town," Jak added. "None seem particularly close to the truth."

Sir Paren wasn't surprised word had gotten out. "Knowing it exists at all is enough to be a problem." He turned to the master of arms. "By the way, Corgos, congratulations on the birth of your daughter. Is Dame Tiana well?"

"Quite well, sir, and thank you. Though my contribution was rather small!"

"Yes, our women do all the work," agreed Paren, taking another swig of his wine. "It seems the Ani knew about it all along."

"They built it," Sir Jak pointed out.

"And the knowledge of it here was passed down to only a few. My brother. Sir Copago. No one ever thought to say anything to me. Yes, they overlooked you too, Corgos, despite you being master of arms."

Corgos had been miffed that his predecessor, Copago, had chosen to impart the knowledge to Donzalo rather than him. He had left Count Bolos out of it, as well. That was all the past now, Copago was master of arms in Paren's own keep and Donzalo even further away.

"Maybe it could be blocked up," suggested Jak. "Some gunpowder in the tunnel might do it."

"If it didn't bring down the whole cliff and the castle atop it," Corgos pointed out.

"That could happen anytime, anyway," said the burly knight.

Paren could only laugh. "Let's not hurry it!" They all raised their cups to that.

"I'll keep a guard posted in it anyway, for now," Corgos said. "Maybe a gate of some sort could be built."

Paren nodded. It was one of many concerns for the weeks and months ahead. "We'll talk about it again," he said. "And we'll have to get Lady Lomela's thoughts."

"Will she rule here now?" asked Corgos. Undoubtedly concerned about his own position, thought Paren.

"The Countess Lomela and I rule as co-regents for the boy. Donzalo is named too, should he choose to return. Yes, I know that is unlikely. In truth, I'll have to be—well, want to be—elsewhere much of the time, so most of it will fall to his mother."

"With Jobareth Nafal at her side, no doubt," spoke Corgos. He didn't quite approve, did he?

"Nafal's a good lad," Jak said. "And smart. But we'll keep an eye on him, eh?" His chuckle was echoed by Paren's. After a few seconds, Corgos smiled as well.

"That's enough of business," said Paren, stretching his considerable frame in his high-backed chair. "I'm going to be off for my own keep and my own wife before the Yule and I truly am expecting you two to keep an eye on things. Otherwise," he warned, "I would have to send Sir Copago back to run the place and he would not be happy about that at all."

He suspected the pair half-believed him.

~ ~ ~

"Do you speak from afar?"

Lady Se appeared uncertain how to respond for a moment. Then she clearly made some sort of decision. "I know how but rarely use the knowledge. Your father taught me. I was ignorant of it before him."

"My father taught me too. He's the only one I've ever spoken to and—and I'm not sure if I know enough to safely speak with others."

"But you know how to ward yourself."

"Yes, I can do that quite well. No one's getting through my walls!" Fachalana might have come close to giggling. "But someone pokes at them now and again. I think I need to practice before opening myself up."

"With me? I may be no better at it than you." Se frowned. "Or not as good. It's a somewhat common skill among sorcerers, I know, but some are better than others, and some can't manage it at all. Like my Guesare. He never could get the trick of it."

"But he was able to sense many things. I remember that of him."

"Yes, wordless things. My son was more about feelings than words, despite being a bard."

Fachalana thought it best not to pursue the subject. Se was not the person to practice with. "I'll not worry about it for now," she said. "I've much more to concern myself with."

Se seemingly accepted this and speaking from afar was dropped. She'll remember it, though, Fachalana told herself.

She did have her father's knowledge in her head, knowledge still somewhat a jumble but on which she could draw. She had set it apart, so to speak, and did not like delving too deeply into it. But she would have to someday, wouldn't she? That might be part of her healing.

Speaking from afar was not so complicated, in theory. One sent a part of ones self to another world, another universe, to speak to another who had done the same. There were an infinite number of little pocket universes where one might do such things. If she could learn enough, if she could be certain she would be safe.

From there, who could say? There was an infinite existence she could explore, should she choose. Oh, there was someone knocking again. Go away! But he wouldn't hear as long as she kept her wards up. Or she. Fachalana couldn't even tell that.

Maybe it was time she rested again in that Plain of Silver and tried to sort things out. What better place to seek into what had been her father, the memories that had come from his mind to hers when they shared one space, one consciousness?

"That's beautiful, Se," she said aloud. "I'm afraid I never learned to embroider."

The priestess smiled. "And I never learned to fence, my lady, but I've heard you do it quite beautifully."

"Ah, but at least you've never killed anyone with your embroidery." With that she rose, nodded a farewell, and returned to her own chamber.

~ ~ ~

Little villages lay along their route, villages where the traders were happy to stop an hour, an afternoon, and make some sales. There seemed to be no hurry.

East they were traveling, skirting a spur of the mountains. "We'll meander around a bit, with an aim to ending up at Tod-ford for the Yule," Godos was told. "A good place to be on a big holiday like that, when folks come from all over." He wasn't completely sure how long it was until the Yule. Three weeks? Somewhere around that.

The note to his home could be sent from Tod-ford too. For the first time, he missed that home. He had intended to be there for the holiday, no matter what plans his parents were making for him. Celatas was never more alive than at the Yule. To be at the family mansion looking down over the lights of the capital! It was a modest mansion to be sure, for even the richest merchants knew not to flaunt their wealth before the old aristocracy, but there were few better located, high on the hills behind the city. Nearly as high as the king's keep itself! One could see a great expanse of the River Chas, as far as the bend below town and extending into misty distance above it. The Chas was still a mighty river at Celatas and large vessels made their way up to the city's wharves, some all the way from the sea. The King's Bridge could be seen spanning it, the bridge Lareth had built on great stone piles, the furthest down the river of any crossing.

Instead, he was here in a scrubby rolling land populated chiefly by piebald cattle, selling pots to the leathery wives of leathery cowherds. The daughters were not quite so leathery and more than one caught his eye.

As he caught their eyes. Indeed, young Godos had a bit of gift for attracting women of all ages to any display he stood near. Galaro saw this at once and made the most of it. "Talk to them," he told the boy. "It needn't be about the merchandise. We can handle that end of it." Then, almost as an afterthought, "But do be careful of their men folk. We don't want any blood spattered on our goods, you know."

He thought of replying it would be their blood but also thought better of it. Godos Tasetha was acquiring wisdom.

~ ~ ~

Fachalana was half-asleep, curled on a couch in one of the halls in Drolwym. There had been some sort of party for someone and food and noise and Blen didn't seem to be around or anyone else.

What was that? Another world, somehow, impinging on her awareness. Casurru! He was daydreaming and was inadvertently, unconsciously, entering that other world. Wasn't that how Father discovered Benawis's talents? Ugh, Benawis! Such a nasty man.

Casurru.

Huh?

He was rightly startled, confused. *It is Fachalana. We are speaking from afar.*

64

Huh? again.

You have wizard powers, she told him. *I noticed you drifting into another world without knowing it, and followed you.*

I—I. The boy broke off. Back in their own world and that was probably as well. He stared at her from across the room. Maybe he thought it was all a dream. A fantasy.

Well, she'd best make sure he knew it was reality. Fachalana beckoned the boy to her, motioned him to sit at her side. "Do you understand what just happened?"

A vigorous shake of the head.

"You knew it was possible you might have abilities. I'm sure someone has mentioned it."

"Uh, yes. And I do? I mean, really?"

"Not a doubt. You're going to have to learn about them now. Lady Se could help you."

He gave her a sly look. "I'd rather you did."

"Hmm, maybe sometimes." But she knew it was a bad idea as soon as she said it. She could barely help herself, much less this novice. "Yes, sometimes. But Se first." She spied the thane's wife across the room. "Right now, in fact. Come on."

It didn't take long to fill her in. There wasn't that much filling in to do. Se nodded wisely. She was very good at doing that, thought Fachalana. "We're going to have to begin training Guesare's daughter too," she said. "Perhaps the two together." One couldn't help telling Casurru didn't much like that idea.

"And you must help us with it," Se added.

The boy brightened up considerably at that.

11

"There is a real possibility our child will be born on the Yule," Prince Modareth told his brother. They sat before a roaring fire in a chamber in their father's keep, towering above the capital city. Modareth's private rooms, they were, for Gawis had come seeking him.

"Some children are," allowed Gawis. He then figured up some dates in his head. "I say, you must have gone right to work after your marriage." He was absolutely certain nothing went on between Modareth and Carrana before.

"We did our best. But that's largely luck, you know."

Indeed it was. Or forces beyond human control, which came to the same thing. Those sorts of thoughts had been in the crown prince's head lately. His own wife was pregnant again and luck or forces or whatever would determine whether he finally had a male heir.

Before then he would learn what gender his half-brother's offspring might be. Scrawny, shy Modareth, with his shock of black hair, so different from the sturdy, sandy-blond Gawis. And so much smarter, he knew.

It was to pick those brains of Modareth he had come here, though, admittedly, the boy always seemed to have the best wine in the place. He sipped a little of it now. Their own father had advised him to use his brother for counsel. Someday he would be king. He needed such men at his side and on his side.

"I keep hearing about the Partanacan situation," he said. "A union between them and the Coradeans, right?"

Modareth nodded.

"But they were united once." This he knew from the histories, little though he paid attention to them as a lad.

"That is so. A couple of centuries ago—I could look up the date but I don't think it matters." The room was lined with bookshelves so the prince most certainly could.

"It does not," agreed Gawis. "Tell me about it. If there's one thing I know you can lecture about, it is history."

Modareth smiled an acknowledgment. He knew he could wax pedantic and probably enjoyed it. "A couple of centuries ago there was a union of the Coradean and Partanacan empires. The emperor was actually a Coradean, invited to fill the empty Partanacan throne, but Partanacan interests soon took precedence in the administration."

"He was named emperor of both, right? They were still officially two nations."

"True. Many Coradeans soon felt they had gotten the worst of the deal and there was ongoing unrest. This came to a head when the Ani invaded Lorj, and the emperor, in his far-off southern capital, did not send aid. In his defense, his troops were busy fighting Ani elsewhere, but it seemed Lorj was of low priority. He might have given it up as a lost cause."

"But the Ani never conquered Lorj. That I know."

"No, the Lorjam, both the Coradean north and the Partanacan south, united under their marshal and drove them back to the mainland."

"I've been told they had over-extended themselves. Maybe by you! And there was disease?"

"Yes, plague. That hurt the Ani here too, and in Lama. In Lorj, after their victory, most did not wish to welcome the return of imperial rule and Lorj declared its independence under the marshal. The Partancans did hold onto the far south and the borders shifted back and forth from time to time but they have remained unable to reconquer the island. Until now. Conquest through diplomacy."

"The Lorjam are inviting the Partanacan emperor back."

"They are considering it. As Coradean emperor in the north and in the Coradean holdings on the mainland, with promises of remaining independent. There are similar promises to the south, though they would become Partanacan, as of old.

"I understand the marshal is actually the architect of it all. Perhaps he feels the nations will be stronger reunited."

"Hmm. They may well be, and a greater threat to Sharsh, but like two brothers under the same roof, they may take to fighting again, don't you think?"

Modareth laughed quite long. "I think, Brother," he choked out at last, "you are far wiser than some give you credit for."

~ ~ ~

"Gloomy here," remarked Jobareth.

"That it is. We're not far from where Radal's men ambushed us last spring."

When this man was conducting Donzalo back to his home. The place that might become his own home now. Two riders on a nearly empty highway, they were, swampland lying close on their right, extending to the unseen Weldar. Traffic had thinned considerably as they journeyed south along the Great Road. It should pick up again when they got past this stretch. But slow it would remain everywhere in this season.

"We're making good time," he said, just to have something to say. He might well have made the same remark before.

"Good enough." Habidros allowed, looking about. "I may never travel this way again, Nafal. My home will be in the south and the Cuddon only a memory."

"Not to mention the Siphic States." The knight had spent much of his adult life there, in the service of one city-state or another.

"Those I do not think I will miss, though I'll have many a memory of them too." Habidros laugh. "And many a tale to tell my children and grandchildren. There will also be many of those!"

Jobareth hoped his bride felt the same about it. "Donni's great-grandfather went off to the Siphic States as a mercenary, it is said."

"A noted condottiere and remembered still. Statues were raised to him and mobs haven't pulled all of them down yet."

"That sort of thing happens?"

"It's an everyday occurrence. Those Siphics can be a discontented lot. That's why there was always plenty of work for those like me. Some keep at it too long."

It was hard to read what his thoughts were on that. Regret or relief for having put the life behind him? Some of each, maybe.

"Old Paren settled down as one of the landed gentry eventually," continued the Cuddonian. "I've met some of his descendants."

"And now you're doing something of the same sort."

"So I am. This is the spot. Their captain had musketeers in the trees over there and then charged us on horse. We might not have made it out had not my brother shown up."

"Galaro." Jobareth had met the man at the great Summer Fair at Ros-town. "Any idea where he is now?"

"Somewhere he can make a profit. Beyond that, I can't guess."

~ ~ ~

"It's awfully flat, isn't it?" Godos had never seen such an expanse of absolutely level land.

"When it rains here, the water doesn't know which way to run," one of the traders informed him. Godos smiled an appreciation of her joke. It *was* very flat, with farm fields extending on both sides of the road. They had traveled east almost as far as the River Weldar.

"Over that way lies Todmouth," said the woman. "We won't be

going there. That's a good thing 'cause the men tend to misbehave themselves in that cesspool of a town."

"That they do," agreed her friend. "Now we've hit the main road we'll travel back west to Tod-ford, alongside the river."

"More or less."

Godos Tasetha knew of Tod-ford or at least had heard it mentioned in the family home. The seat of Count Orgelo, the most powerful lord of southern Lama, and a man whose business interests rarely were in accord with theirs. He trafficked with smugglers, it was said, and Godos was seeing the reality of it.

"Are we in County Arvaram?" he asked.

The women weren't sure. "Near the border, that's for sure. They don't bother with much of a guard there. Too much to keep an eye on."

"Aye, but there are always patrols. Chances are they know about us by now."

"They all know Galaro. We'll get no grief from them."

"And the count's niece is marrying Galaro's brother."

It was the first he'd heard of it. Certainly the captain had said nothing. But then he rarely talked of himself and never of any family.

"This brother is at Tod-ford?"

They weren't sure. "I've heard he rode off with Sorsen—that's Orgelo's son—to chase bandits. No news since then, or none Galaro's been willing to share."

"Looks like we're stopping at this village. Get ready to get to work, boy."

12

"I couldn't travel all the way to the capital, of course," Oder told them, "but I went far enough to speak with the Margrave of the West. On my recommendation, he approves of Donzalo taking up a lordship in the Cuddon."

Vantare seemed amused. "Lordship? I suppose one could call it that, though no Cuddonian would."

"Your brother is revealing more of his true self," Donzalo whispered in Ansa's ear. "He'll never be able to pass himself off as a wandering bard again."

"He told me he was going to put that aside. Whether to retire to his estates or move to a higher position in the imperial service, he has yet to decide."

Donzalo wondered about those estates. He had but the vaguest idea about the siblings' status in the Anian Empire but knew they were of a powerful noble family. Oder wore the title of jarl in his homeland. Was Ansa truly willing to live in a tumbling-down little keep in the hills with him?

"And what say the Cuddonians to Donzalo's not-a-lordship?" asked the Ani.

"The Cuddonians are not so sure yet. Most seem willing to give a begrudging assent."

"And for Cuddonians that is the equivalent of overwhelming approval," Lady Se added.

Se was not to be denied a voice in this meeting. Nor was Mausare, who had ridden over from his farmstead. It was close, much closer than those of Ourru and Cuelle, which lay a day or more away.

Indeed, pretty much any Cuddonian who happened to find his

way to the room, from laird to stable boy, was entirely free to express an opinion and quite likely to do so.

But neither Ansa nor Donzalo felt inclined to take part. "Guesare looked rather like his father, didn't he?" Ansa now whispered.

He nodded. The minstrel had that same compact frame, the same broad brow. But his hair was of a curling gold as was his mother's, though hers was turning to gray. Jola, too, had such hair, but more a ruddy gold.

He could see the mother in Jola and, yes, Lord Radal. Radal's other daughter was not here, nor Blen. Were they together? Donzalo wished the two would stop holding each other at arms' length. They were as obviously meant for each other as Ansa and he.

Yes, yes, it had taken a little while for them to sort that out. Did someone say his name?

"We were speaking about your name, Donni," the thane told him.

"Oh. I think I should call myself Rosam no longer if I am to be of the Cuddon."

"So feel we too. Have you another in mind?"

His hand went to the silver brooch at his shoulder, the brooch in the shape of a wolf given him by the fay. It had proven a useful talisman in his battle against Radal and he had taken the wolf as his emblem. Though he had lent it a while to Fachalana in her need, she had returned it after dreaming in the cavern. Donzalo now wore it again himself.

"Our friend Arsel's name means 'wolf-friend.' It is one of the names he wears but not his true name, the name only the elves know."

"He told it to Jola," Se commented.

Yes, he knew that. "It is a good name but it is his name. How might one say something similar in Krevod?

"Maybe felesar," suggested Vantare.

72

"Or felean," Se said.

Mausare spoke. "Felewym would be wolf-home. That should be name of your keep."

"I like that," said Ansa.

Donzalo did too.

"The Laird of Felewym. It has a nice ring to it," felt the thane. "Now all we need is to get you two married so you can fill your new home with a family."

"We could do it right now, with your brother here," he told Ansa.

She looked up at Vantare. "How soon can you get your priest of Jov here?"

"Will tomorrow do?"

~ ~ ~

"Well, it's all up to me now, it seems," remarked Countess Lomela, watching Sir Paren and his entourage wind out of the court-yard and through the inner gate. At least until Jobareth arrives, she added silently. When will any further word come from the Cuddon?

"You have Jak and me, my lady," Traspa reminded her. She stood close behind, holding young Ros in her arms. The boy's eyes were fixed on the activity below the balcony, though he spoke no words.

"Yes, I know. I want Jak to stay busy with the rebuilding Paren began. He'll know how it's to be done."

"And he and Sir Corgos won't get in each other's way if he has a task, my lady?"

"Something like that," she laughed. "It's warm today. Warm for the season." The weather here did not differ so much from that of Celatas; both had mild winters and hot summers. Back in Sharsh, she might have spent those summers in the mountains. But it was drier here, with the mountains between them and the sea. Snow was rare at Castle Rosam. At least Lomela had seen little in the few winters she had resided there.

"You're the count now," she said, addressing Ros. "Maybe I should send you to hold audiences and I could be the one who naps."

In fact, why not? "Bring the boy along while I go speak with the ambassador," she told Traspa. "It can be his first official act as Count Ros. Would you like to see Lord Doufan, Ros?"

"Fawn," he replied.

"Yes, Fawn.

"No." Then the child giggled.

"He's just being contrary for the fun of it," declared Traspa.

"Would that I could get away with it. Come along anyway; I'm sure Lord Doufan would be glad to see you no matter how naughty you are."

Traspa smirked. "Doufan can be pretty naughty too, my lady."

"Then let's go see what mischief he is up to."

But it would only be dreary letters and diplomatic requests and points about County Rosam's relations with its neighbors. At least Doufan was still here to talk to her; too soon, he would leave as well.

~ ~ ~

"I'm Nel," announced the girl. She was perhaps twelve and was Guesare's daughter. She looked it too.

Her mother was slender and boyish. Boyish enough to appeal to Guesare, apparently! Shy, too. She offered no name but Se introduced her as Fausala.

"She's intimidated by you," Se told her later. "As are many. You are reputed to be a great sorceress and—well, people think of my daughter when they see you."

"She's one of your priestesses?"

"She is. Donzalo would have met her but I doubt he remembered

74

the name." A slightly sad smile. "And I doubt my son would have mentioned her to him."

So they had begun Nel's lessons and those of Casurru, she and Se, and Fausala as well. The girl had apparently just begun to show her abilities, though it had been known she would have them. Much earlier than Fachalana. She had been in her twenties before she—or her father—had any inkling she was a sorceress.

"The first thing to learn and the most important thing," Fachalana had announced to the two students, "is to be able to ward yourself. If you can not block out dangers, all else is useless."

"Mom taught me some of that," volunteered Nel.

That was good. They worked on it a little while—long sessions were not a good idea—with plans to continue the lessons. It was on the second day that Fachalana inadvertently let her own guard slip.

Fachalana, isn't it? came a voice, a deep masculine voice, though such things could be deceiving when speaking from afar.

She could have blocked him right then. Easily. She did have the power, she did have the knowledge. Yet there was something familiar about that voice, something that woke a memory. Intrigued, she answered. *It is. And who might you be?*

Call me Axacles. You are the one who upset our plan to assassinate Prince Modareth. I have never understood how you knew of it.

Oh, that's who this wizard was. *I heard you speaking with your agent in Celatas. In a dream.*

There was a long silence. *You have great power. You are indeed your father's daughter. But—I would hope you are not drawn into the darkness as was he.*

Fachalana was not able to stifle her laugh. *And you are all goodness?*

To her surprise, the sorcerer laughed with her. *I serve my emperor, not darkness. I am told the prince should die, I pass on orders to make it so.*

He peered at her. She could see him clearly, a dark man, but plump rather than ascetic like her father. *Yet somehow, it was not made so.*

Indeed it was not. Modareth is my friend. They had grown up together.

And he is no longer a target. Admittedly, such things can change. With both his wife and that of Prince Gawis pregnant, things are being rethought.

It was stupid to try to kill Modi. You may tell the emperor that for me.

Hmm, not the best career choice for me, my lady. For that matter, it is probably not a good idea for me to speak with you; some might read treason into such conversations. But allow me to warn you—there are powerful sorcerers out there who are a danger to you. You have been noticed and some might wish to use you and some might wish to destroy you. With that pleasant thought I will bid you a good bye.

The Partanacan wizard faded and Fachalana returned to the room in Drolwym. "You were talking afar to someone, weren't you?" spouted Nel at once.

Se and Fausala were staring at her. Casurru just looked confused.

"I was," she reported, "and I think it was a good thing." She had learned from it. "But I may not again anytime soon."

Not until she had more of her father's knowledge, both that within and that in his books back in Sharsh. Fachalana had not thought of those in some time but now she ached to return and read them. To learn! That was what she needed.

"More lessons tomorrow," announced Se. "Wine now."

Fachalana thought that a pretty good idea.

13

A TROOP OF horsemen galloped toward them across the field, lancers, in tunics of blue and white. The sun shone but dully on blackened breastplates. Galaro held up a hand to signal a halt.

"Ho, Galaro!" A dark-haired man doffed his helmet and trotted up to greet him. He was large but not as large as the Cuddonian. "We heard a band of vagrants was wandering the county!"

"Only honest peddlers, Sir Sorsen."

"As honest as most, I suppose." Sorsen laughed at his jest and went on. "Have you heard any news of your brother? His wife-to-be is getting antsy."

"Nay, we've come from the south and have had no news of any sort in some time. The last we heard Habidros was chasing bandits with you."

Sorsen fell in beside Galaro as the column of traders began again to move down the road. His troop rode along on their flank. "The chasing of bandits turned into much more. That wizard Radal captured Keep Rosam and they killed the count—Bolos that is—and we had to mount a rescue and Habidros went off to the Cuddon for some reason I couldn't quite understand. But he's a good fellow and I figured it was best he did it now instead of after he was married to my cousin!"

"I suspect there is somewhat more to that story," remarked Galaro, "and I'll get it from someone sometime. Maybe from Habi."

"We hope he'll be back for the Yule. That your plan, Galaro?"

"With your father's permission, we would like to set up at Todford for the holidays. Until then, we shall make our way along this road, selling a few trinkets here and there."

"I think we'll all be happy enough to see you and your traders.

Just don't break out those bagpipes of yours! At least, their playing is not among Habi's vices."

"But how else would a Cuddonian greet the return of the sun on Yule morn? Oh." He turned and waved Godos to him. "This young fellow is very far from his home and fears his parents think him dead. Do you think we could send a letter to Celatas from your home?"

Sorsen looked him over. "Don't see why not. Sharshite, eh? We won't hold that against you!"

"His father is somewhat important. Fronos Tasetha."

Sir Sorsen whistled. "We'd just heard his son was lost at sea. That sort of news travels fast, even to here. Hmm, Dad might have thoughts on having a Tasetha around."

"Count Orgelo would see all sorts of opportunities. I suspect he'd make the boy an honored guest."

"Ha, until he forgot about him. He has a way of doing that. But you're right. Why don't you come along with us right now, lad? Galaro will catch up to you in a couple weeks."

Godos glanced toward Galaro. He was more than uncertain about riding off with this man.

The Cuddonian nodded. "You can even borrow that nag until then. Oh, but if you send a letter, tell them to write you at Ros-town," advised Galaro. "We intend to get there and if we don't, you can go on to the place yourself."

A few minutes later he was riding with the cavalry of County Arvaram, headed north along the red dirt road to Tod-ford.

~ ~ ~

"I never did expect those two to make it all the way to the Yule, married or not," confided Se. "Now when will it be for you and Blen?"

Fachalana gave thanks that her complexion would help hide her blush. "We have not spoken of such things," she blurted.

"Oh?" The priestess considered this. "And which of you is the reason for that?"

She could only shrug and make no answer. She knew no answer. She didn't want to try to think of one. This was Ansa's day, hers and Donzalo's. Oh, the priest was addressing the couple. "Donzalo Felean," he said. When had they decided on that name? No one told her anything! Something about becoming one with Ansa. And then the same with her.

"Ansa Vikon." Was that her family name? She'd never heard it before either. But she would bet it was known in Sharsh by people in high places, if Ansa's family really was important. She might inquire when she got back. Discreetly.

Maybe they could go now. She was stronger, wasn't she? As soon as she asked herself, Fachalana knew the answer. More time was needed. Maybe after the Yule. Until then—what? Sit around Drolwym with Blen? It really wasn't so unattractive an idea.

And visit again on the Silver Plain. That was a part of her healing. Husband and wife! The priest had called the blessings of Jov and Esefa on them and was sending them forth to the world. That was something new. She'd never heard it said at a wedding in Sharsh, despite having the same gods.

Fachalana felt she was being sent forth too, but not as a wife. That was it, wasn't it? There was still something she needed to do. Blen might have a part in it. She hoped he had a part in it.

Oh, they were quite literally sending the couple forth, out the front doors of Drolwym! But only for a moment; they kissed and ran back inside, tracking snow in behind them. Now for the feast and dancing and she felt suddenly tired. So tired—no one would miss her too much, would they?

Fachalana, the Viscountess Ildoram, slipped away and found her bed.

~ ~ ~

Lareth of Sharsh looked out over his city. Misty rain obscured, softened the view. Winter rain; that was more common here than snow. Lights shone everywhere below, on the streets, on his bridge, even across the river, though those were barely to be made out.

He was alone. His mistress had been here a while and they had talked. The Lady Lis was intelligent and could converse on many things—politics included—but he missed the evenings he spent with his old friend Radal. Yes, despite his betrayal, he wished he were here with him right now.

There would be no other in his lifetime to replace him. Lareth was not young, though there was no reason to believe he would die anytime soon. He might go twenty, even thirty years more. Or he could fall off his horse and break his neck tomorrow. "Remember to stay off horses," he mumbled to himself and snickered.

Only a couple weeks to the Yule celebrations. Balls he would be expected to attend. Oh, he would probably enjoy them well enough once he got there. He still liked to dance with the young ladies and make Lis jealous.

And yes, sometimes he cheated on her, as he had on both his wives. Maybe he should just go ahead and marry the woman, despite the politics. Everyone knew he was never going to marry anyone else.

And Gawis would very much appreciate it if he didn't marry a young woman who might provide heirs.

Doufan would be back eventually. Doufan he could trust but he was not Radal. He would never give himself wholeheartedly to the king as had his friend and protege. There was something guarded about Doufan. That made him a very good diplomat as well as a useful spy. Young Blen had something of the same about him. Was he still off in the Cuddon? Yes, yes, with Radal's daughter. Lomela herself had written a letter about all that. Between her words and Doufan's he had a good understanding of all that had happened at Castle Rosam.

The future political situation there was not so clear. Young Nafal was going to stay and serve his daughter? He'd always worshiped the girl; Lareth had recognized that when they were barely more than toddlers. He would serve her well—serve her and not Sharsh. Lomela would surely have the sense to marry the boy, after a suitable period of mourning.

Of all his children—ah, his legitimate children—she was the most alike to him. It was too bad she couldn't sit the throne of Sharsh. He could only hope that Gawis continued in the growth he had shown.

And that his wife would bear him a son and heir this spring.

~ ~ ~

"It was speaking from afar, I think, that tired her so," opined Se. "She might not have realized it at the time."

"But not just that," Fausala said.

"No, I suppose not. Ansa was disappointed but may have understood better than any." Se snickered. "And I'm sure Donzalo didn't disappoint her."

"If she gets tired of him, she can send him to one of us," said another priestess.

"Or all of us." The women raised their goblets to this.

"Better you all get home to your own husbands," said Se. "Even you, Fausala."

"Not to mention all those young ones."

"The terrors of Drolwym!"

"Oh, but Fausi was quite a terror herself at that age."

"I still am," she informed them.

"But it is nearly dawn," said one. "Se's right. There's supposed to be a dawn blessing, right?"

"Optional but it is in the tradition. A blessing at their door after the first night together."

"Okay, let's head—um, where is their room, anyway?"

"Somewhere upstairs?"

"Ah, too much trouble. Let Se attend to it."

And with that, one by one, the priestesses of Rema went to find their husbands and their beds. It is likely most of them chose to sleep.

14

HERE THERE WAS peace. Fachalana sat on the temple steps, resting, not yet ready to delve into herself. But this was the place to do it, she was sure. This was the place to at least make a beginning.

But she was not meant to hide here. She would have to move beyond, in time. Where? That was what she needed to learn.

Fachalana.

It was a voice she had heard before, a liquid female voice that had named itself both Jola and Diba. *I'm here. But who are you? Diba?*

Yes. I am Diba the Huntress. But there is also something of Jola in me.

How is that?

Jola and I became one, to stand against Nosana when the Lady of the Dark Moon possessed her.

As Asak possessed my father. I understand this.

Even so. A part of her remains with me; not Jola, for she has flown, but her memories.

This too Fachalana understood. She held her father's memories.

If you become one with us, you can share in this. Then none can stand against thee.

I am not my sister. I believe—I believe I have my own way.

This may be so. Yet the offer remains, for you are beloved of us. As is Donzalo.

Donzalo? That was understandable. Jola loved him and he loved Jola. *But he is not mine.*

There seemed a long pause, though it was difficult to judge such things here. *You fought beside him once, fought for his life against your own father.*

I did. Donzalo is wed to my friend and I love them both.

Ansa. She can not share what we offer.

And I think I can not take what you offer.

There came a golden laugh. *Maybe so, Fachalana. Even goddesses may be frustrated by the turns of destiny.*

Fachalana waited long but the goddess spoke no more. In time, she returned to Drolwym.

~ ~ ~

"The king," spoke Lord Doufan, "wishes me to escort the Viscountess Fachalana home. If possible."

"So you'll stay here until she returns?"

"So it seems, my lady, if it takes not too long. Your father may become impatient." He suspected the order had come as something of a whim of Lareth. It was the sort of thing his monarch came up with when he sat and brooded.

"There may or may not be a new ambassador sent out before then. Without Blen here, I can not leave the embassy with no one in charge." No need to mention Jobareth Nafal. He was no longer in the service of Sharsh.

Lomela gave a knowing smile. "Where Fachalana goes it is likely Blen will too."

So he wasn't the only one to notice. "I would think that so, my lady. Your father also informed me Radal's remains have been interred at his country estate."

"He writes you letters?"

"Yes. I think he has no one else to confide in. Save you, of course."

Lomela seemed to think on that for an uncomfortably long time. "He has no one since Radal's death. Do you think he sees Radal's daughter as someone to take his place?"

"It has crossed my mind. I think he could do worse than to have Lady Fachalana near." There was no more business to discuss, but the diplomat was in no hurry to leave Castle Rosam. Sitting in the embassy bored him and he'd explored Ros-town thoroughly. "Our young count is not holding audience today?"

"He was rather unruly the last time."

"Ros is an active little man, isn't he? He reminds me of your father, my lady. His hair was that color when he was young." He might have said he also reminded him of the boy's father but chose not to. Both were aware he knew of the young count's true paternity but Doufan was nothing if not discreet.

"But my father has never attempted to climb the drapes. At least not when I was about!"

"I would think not. Yet I have heard he climbed to a few balconies when young."

Lomela sobered. "While Radal held the horses. He was truly devoted to my father."

"An unhealthy devotion." Doufan was willing to speak his mind on this. Speak it vehemently, even. "And in the end it all fell to ruin."

The countess cocked her head, regarded the man for a few seconds. "So you can feel strongly about things."

Doufan shrugged. "We all have our weaknesses, my lady."

~ ~ ~

"Donzalo." He looked up from his book. "May we speak?"

"Certainly, Fachalana." He put the book aside and motioned toward a chair.

"You have walked on the Plain of Silver as I have. And you knew Jola and, in a sense, even Diba. I know not anyone better to speak to of—of what I have seen there."

She was surprised by the sudden gravity of his expression. "Then tell me of it, my lady."

Her tale of her encounter, of Diba's words, poured out of her. All that she could remember, even those that discomforted her. Or Donzalo, for that matter.

When she came to an end, he nodded and sat thinking for some time. Fachalana felt it best to wait.

"I have thought much of that battle we fought together, but things rushed by since and I never spoke aught of it," he said at last. "I saw what is within you, that night, and it had nothing to do with Diba or Jola. It was a great golden bird, a fiery eagle."

Fachalana tried to look within herself. Was this so?

"I recognized it from my reading. It is the Firebird, the emblem of the olden kings of Sharsh, come to them from the heritage of Zedos and to him from the gods who were among his ancestors."

She tried to laugh. "Are you saying I am a god?"

Donzalo smiled in return. "Maybe a demigod. At least you have this heritage. It could have come from your mother."

Yes, her mother did have the blood of the old kings. And this was combined with the heritage of her father. He would never have known of any of it, would he?

"This explains many things," she responded. "And raises many more questions! But at least I know some of the ones I should ask now."

"That is good, then." Donzalo smiled a broad smile. "I am happy you are beloved of Diba. And me too!"

"But poor Ansa is left out."

"I'm not so sure of that. Ansa may have been born a huntress. Haven't you noticed she looks like the statues of Diba?"

From his tone, she knew he wasn't serious. Yet—Ansa did look like those statues of a lithe archer. "Yes, but Ansa is an Ani and worships the sky or something like that."

"No, Ansa is a Cuddonian now, the same as me."

And she would live far away, here in these hills, while Fachalana

—where would she go? Back to Sharsh? She didn't belong anywhere. Maybe not even on the Plain of Silver. She couldn't help herself and began to sob.

Fachalana found herself in her bed the next morning and couldn't remember how she got there.

15

Count Orgelo, as his son had expected, forgot about his young guest after a couple days. Godos did not mind in the least. He could laze about the great log fortress and eat steak all day, if he wished. His letter had duly been dispatched but no one was sure how long it would take to get to Celatas. Maybe it would arrive by the Yule, maybe not.

Godos hoped it would. Letting his parents know he was alive would be a pretty good Yule gift, wouldn't it?

The town and keep of Tod-ford lay, not at all surprisingly, by a ford of the Tod River. The first one above its somewhat distant mouth. The Tod was a wide river, even here, flowing through a rolling countryside of sparse grass and scrub.

A balcony ran all around the big central hall in the fortress. Or house; it seemed more the latter than aught else. Godos leaned against its railing and watched men and women come and go, some eating, some talking, some busy at one sort of work or another. Lots of leather goods came out of Tod-ford. Plain hides too, to be worked elsewhere.

And there were girls, sun-tanned girls with trim figures, girls who rode horses and girls who served in the house and girls who undoubtedly did other things. He'd seen Lenasha, the woman who was supposed to marry Galaro's brother. She didn't look bad either and was said to be quite the horsewoman.

What would his parents think if he brought home a bride from here? Not one of the women they had pointed him toward in Celatas could compare with these. Oh, these were only daydreams.

And it would be quite unfair to take one of them away from this place. Down the wide central stair he slowly made his way—after making sure Sir Sorsen was nowhere about. One was too likely to get caught in that man's wake and dragged along. No, he'd go to the exercise yard and find someone to fence.

Godos had not needed to use his sword in his defense, but was well aware it could happen. It could happen as it did when the traders were attacked and he had been forced to kill a man. It was the first time. The only time.

Sometimes it didn't seem like he was the one who did it at all. It was some other Godos, some dream-Godos. Maybe be didn't feel like fencing right now. What was all this commotion? A crowd was gathering along the road.

"It's Galaro," someone called out. "Galaro and his traders!"

They would surely need help unloading wagons.

~ ~ ~

Again, the Plain of Silver extended all around her. There was no voice of Diba this time. There were no distractions. Fachalana could concentrate on herself, seek within as she had known she must.

So much! And so much of Radal to try to understand. Slowly, cautiously. A shimmering out there? It was hard to make out against the silver haze.

A shadow, the translucent shadow of a man. *Father?* She sensed the truth of it.

Yes. It seemed a whisper in her head.

How? I saw you die.

Die. Yes, I remember dying, falling from the sky. I am dead. But part of me—much of me—was not in our world when I—ended there. It remains here. I remain here, and can not break the bond that holds me.

In the realm of Asak. It seemed the only explanation.

In his realm. In Asak himself.

And if you could escape?

I could truly die and find rest. A hollow chuckle. *Or this version of me*

89

could. His form wavered, sometimes almost invisible, sometimes just on the edge of solidity.

This is the place I pursued you to, so long ago. Or not so long, was it?

It is a place of healing. The fay showed me the way here, as they had Donzalo.

Yes, Donzalo. I remember how I hated him. How I feared he would be your ruin. Radal or his ghost or whatever he was now remained silent for some time. *And at the last, you defended him against me. Are you to be his wife?*

Oh, no, Father. He loves Ansa.

Ansa. Radal seemed to be trying to find a memory. *Your friend the spy.*

Yes. Though I thought once Donzalo was to be my destiny. She hesitated before saying, *My sister dreamed here once.*

The Jola I did not know.

When he spoke no more, Fachalana asked the question that must be asked. *Can I help you, Father? Can you be freed?*

This I doubt. But know, Fachalana, a part of you is trapped here with me. Not bound here as am I, but lost. You need only find it to be whole again.

Find it?

Yes. Seek. And the shadow of Radal faded into the silver light.

~ ~ ~

What was that shouting! Not that merriment was unexpected in this season. Lomela stepped onto her balcony. It had gotten colder, hadn't it? Two riders in the courtyard.

Jobareth, coming before any word of him! And the tall man riding at his side? Could it be Donzalo? The countess hurried inside, wrapped a cloak about her, and practically ran down the stairs. She needn't practice decorum when no one was around, need she?

Not Donni but his cousin, the Cuddonian knight Habidros. Both had dismounted before she reached them.

Jobareth gave her a deep bow. "Might we spend the Yule with you, my lady?"

"You're barely in time. To arrive unannounced on Yule Eve! Perhaps I should send two such disreputable ruffians on their way." She looked them over, hands on hips. "But I suppose you'll say you hurried here."

Habidros grinned at his companion. "I expected this one would have to keep up with me, my lady, but 'twas the opposite way. He was in a great rush to reach Castle Rosam by this day."

And reach her? So like the romantic boy! But it pleased Lomela; there was no denying that.

"And are you here to stay, Lector Nafal?" she asked.

"If you will have me, my lady."

Habidros wore a bit of a smirk. "However, I may tarry but a day or two. My own ladylove awaits me at Tod-ford."

Lomela might have blushed just a little. Perhaps Jobareth did too but they could blame this wind for reddening their cheeks. "Does she know you are on your way, sir?"

"She does not, my lady."

"Then we shall send a message at once. We can't have—Lenasha, isn't it? We can't have Lenasha wondering and worrying too much."

"I thank you, Lady Lomela. I suspect she had done enough of that."

"Or you hope she has," Jobareth told him.

"I had to listen to such attempts at wit all the way here," complained the Cuddonian. "The Lady Fachalana sends her greetings to you, by the way."

"Then she is well again? Let's get in out of the cold. Or do you prefer to see to your horses first?"

"The grooms will do a good enough job," felt Jobareth. "Yes, Fachalana has found healing, though she needs rest. She will remain at Drolwym with the others at least a while. Possibly through the winter."

"They're all well too," added Habidros. "As this fellow should have said right away."

"Yes, and Ansa and Donzalo are to be married. On the morrow unless they felt that was too long to wait."

"Which I strongly suspect they did."

They entered one of the side doors to the great hall. The place was decorated for the feast tomorrow, though servants with ladders were still hanging greenery from the high oak beams. The scent of pine filled the room. "I might have expected Dame Tiana to be super-vising," remarked Jobareth.

"She has an infant daughter to keep her occupied. And isn't Corgos proud!"

Habidros chuckled. "I can imagine. Ha, maybe I can be proud one of these days too."

"I hope that is so, my friend," said Jobareth.

Friend? A good man to have as a friend, Lomela told herself. Jobareth would need friends in the times to come, as would she. As did everyone!

"Let's get you two into a room somewhere," she said. "The place is quite full and you did arrive unannounced, after all, so don't expect much."

"It's better than sleeping by the roadside," said Habidros.

"Yes," agreed Jobareth. "It is my journey's end."

~ ~ ~

One could not see the ceiling of this cavern; not by the light of the handful of torches illuminating it. Once, many had lit up the cave, their flames flickering red against the darkness, the black rock. It had been a mighty coven, that which had served Nosana.

Another led them now, a robed figure looking down upon other robed figures. "Sisters," she began, "all is not lost. On this, the Day of Darkness, before the cursed sun returns, we are powerful. Let us pray for the day it never comes again!"

"For darkness," came a murmured, ragged response. They were a pitiful bunch, broken by their encounter nearly a year ago. Vis had been there among them, one of the few to escape intact.

"A powerful sorceress has come to Drolwym," she told them. "Sister to the hated Jola." Howls erupted. Good, the drugs were having their effect. The bowls had been passed earlier and the witches had drank deeply. "There are voices—" She gestured toward the darkness above them. "That say she might be turned to the ways of darkness, to the service of the Lady of the Dark Moon, to the service of Asak." She let that sink in. "And others that warn she will be used as a weapon against us. We must watch. We must act when the time comes. You who serve in the keep, watch her. We who see beyond this world will watch as well."

But Vis did not wish to turn a potential rival to the darkness. She wanted her dead.

~ ~ ~

"Fachalana seems herself again."

"Still tired though." There was a definite note of concern in Blen's voice.

"She found something of what she sought," Donzalo said. "So I believe. I might have helped her a little in her quest but others must journey with her from here."

"Meaning me." The knight stared into his cup, as if seeking some augury in the dark wine.

"That was rather poetic, Donni," said Ansa, before he could respond. "Did you practice it?"

"Maybe. Don't you know I practice all the pretty speeches I intend to make to you?" He chuckled. "And then forget them when we are together."

Blen smiled at this. Perhaps it was not so different with him at times. "Ansa has no need of fanciful words from you, sir. She is as fine a minstrel as her brother, if not better."

"Still, it is nice to hear them," she said. "Even stuttered and misre-membered. Fachalana will have to join us for the changing of the year after her nap."

"I pray she can," stated Blen. To what gods he prayed, Donzalo did not know, but the man might well need their aid in days to come.

"Perhaps my wife the minstrel can give us a song for this day," he said.

Blen nodded approval to that idea. "You might find her a harp. There is surely one somewhere around Drolwym."

"But I do not need one," she told him, and began to sing.

And now the longest night has come
upon the hills and fields of home;
here by the friendly fireside
we await Yuletide.

STEPHEN BROOKE

The Day of Darkness nearly done,
tomorrow promises the sun;
though Winter's winds yet howl outside,
we await Yuletide.

Air cold and hard, the sky stands dark
and winter trees sleep leafless, stark;
as snow still blankets countryside
we await Yuletide.

Now sing the carol, drink the health,
the gold of dawn shall be our wealth;
here by the warming hearth inside
we await Yuletide.

Of Mothers: the Second Tale

1

In the land of Lama, the great valley of the River Weldar, they would celebrate the Yule today. In the hills of the Cuddon, too, there would be festivity, and across the mountains in Sharsh.

The Lamans would offer prayer to Kamat, the great god of light, the god of Being, who again triumphed over the Void. That it was only symbolic and that Kamat was far greater than the returning sun, they knew, but it was a good symbol and worth the celebrating.

Elsewhere, different gods were honored. The feasting, however, was just as merry and the gifts as plentiful. There would be kisses beneath the greenery suspended in every threshold. There would be young women in the arms of young men, dreaming before the Yule log. Women and men not so young, as well.

Let the cold winds blow. The midwinter had come and the wheel of the heavens turned on. Spring would follow, and other feasts, on other days.

~ ~ ~

"We shouldn't have to work so hard on a holiday," groused Godos.

"It's the life of a trader," his comrade told him. "Or that of a servant, for that matter. Now lets get these boxes over to the tents."

It was the life of a servant, wasn't it? He'd never thought much about that. Many people worked hard on the Yule and other days so those like his own family could celebrate.

He grumbled now but Godos enjoyed working in the market-place, once everything was set up. There were several tents, some with one trader's goods, some with those of two or three. Each trader was independent, though they followed Galaro's leadership, and each had his or her own wares to sell.

Yet there was some sort of agreement to share profits and costs. That did not interest him so much. Speaking with customers, flirting and flattering and, yes, actually helping them, was what he liked. He had a vague idea that his father did something similar but it certainly wasn't as much fun.

Galaro himself came over. "The competition," he said, nodding toward another group setting up not so far away. It would have been unrealistic to think Galaro was the only trader in the south. The newcomers had but two tents.

"I wonder what they have to sell," he said.

"One of them is a wine seller. That doesn't cut into any profits of ours."

Yes, he could see the kegs. "In Sharsh, they have started putting wine in glass bottles."

"So I heard from Jobareth Nafal."

"Nafal? I know the family." Knew of them, mostly. "The most important wine merchants in all Sharsh." Not to mention having expanded into banking. "Jobareth is a diplomat, isn't he?"

"Aye. He was stationed in County Rosam but I know not whether he is still. If we get there I suppose we'll find out." Galaro ambled off to mind his own tent.

Godos's companion watched him for a moment. "One can not see his sorrow but it is there."

Sorrow? He turned, seeking an explanation. "His brother was slain in those troubles at Castle Rosam. He only learned of it when we arrived here and he got the full story." The man shook his head.

"That dolt Sorsen didn't think to say anything of it when we met on the road."

"The one who was going get married?"

"No, another. A minstrel named Guesare. I met him this past year."

It would be best he not say anything either. Godos picked up another box and toted it toward the tents.

~ ~ ~

The dancing was old fashioned, to say the least. But lively! Fachalana would have kept at it all night had her friends not insisted she rest.

There were viols and flutes and drums and bagpipes. Not one rebec, though, as Guesare had played. Maybe he learned it somewhere else. From Oder, maybe? The Ani had disappeared from Drolwym again, not long after his sister's wedding. No one expected him to return soon.

Blen sat beside her. "I like this better than the music I've heard lately at home," he announced. "It's too complicated."

Home? "And where is home, sir?" she asked him.

He seemed to struggle with finding an answer. "I suppose I mean Sharsh, my lady."

"Yes. I would have to say the same. We'll return someday, won't we? Even if the music does bewilder you." She quite understood what he meant by that. The complex interweaving of melodies had become all the style, and more complex with each year. Fachalana, as any young lady of breeding, had taken lessons in music.

Despite a lack of talent she could hammer away at a virginal with the best of them. "You should hear the Princess Mara play her dulcimer someday," she told her companion. "It is quite beautiful. Even I can tell that!"

"Would I ever be likely to have the opportunity?"

"I could sneak you in Lareth's back door sometime."

"No need," said Donzalo, taking a place beyond Blen. Ansa settled beside him. "Ask your old friend Pol to introduce you. Jobareth told me he is intimate with all the royal family now."

"*And* he took over my theater!" Which she didn't mind. Better than it sitting empty. Did she have any interest in ever running it again? Or being on stage herself? That seemed so distant a life, yet it was her passion less than a year ago.

Ansa was on her feet. "Another gigue! Come on, Donni."

"I'm worn out. Make Blen dance this one. You tell him to, Fachalana."

"Yes. Go," she said, giving the knight a shove. He did as told without a word.

"He's quite obedient, isn't he?" remarked Donzalo.

"He dances the gigue better than you, as well. I think our Blen likes to dance." She gave the tall man at her side a look. "You, not so much."

"Not the lively ones, anyway."

"Oh, you prefer something stately. That would work well with your height, wouldn't it? You and I must dance if there is a pavan. We would impress everyone."

"I doubt these Cuddonian musicians know a pavan. Blen does move well, doesn't he? One might think he would be a better fencer."

Fachalana shook her head. "He's not inclined to improvise or react to his opponent. Blen is a man of discipline and order."

"Oh? I suppose that's true. Then you lack discipline, my lady?" He said it with a smile, but perhaps there was a serious question behind it.

"It is my great failing, Donzalo. Acting helped teach me discipline; without that I might have become completely lost when—well, when I found I had a differen talent."

A little girl climbed into Donzalo's chair and snuggled close to him. "Good evening, Darsena. Escaped your mom and dad again? Lanta and Mausare's daughter," he explained to Fachalana. "They do let children run about everywhere in Drolwym."

"Stay wi' Unc Donni," Darsena proclaimed.

"And they don't in Laman homes or at least not in Castle Rosam," said Fachalana. "I noticed that when I stayed there. We're a lot more like Cuddonians back in Sharsh."

"I suppose I must spoil my many children, if I'm to be a Cuddonian."

She smiled not only at the jest but at the thought of those children. "You'll need to discuss that with Ansa. Who knows what child rearing customs the Ani have?" Fachalana had no idea herself and suspected Donzalo was equally ignorant. But he would know other things. "When do you think you will leave here?"

"Not until you are strong enough to go with us. We've all agreed on that, haven't we?" That was no real answer though. She wanted dates! Donzalo might have seen that in her face. "The winter has set in now too. It is not good weather for travel. Perhaps around the Feast of Awakening. Six weeks, if you feel ready."

"I guess that's the best I'm going to get from you. Oh, they are playing a pavan! On your feet, Sir Donzalo."

And if they didn't impress, at least they didn't embarrass themselves.

~ ~ ~

"Lanesha can wait an extra day," decided Habidros. "I'll stay the morrow." In truth, he could use the rest. It had been a hard ride to the Rosam keep and he needn't hurry on this last leg of his journey.

Plus, he much enjoyed the hospitality of the castle. The Cuddonian had served here a short while, bodyguard to Donzalo, and had not Count Borrago been assassinated he might have been here still. It had been a good post, more so as he liked his cousin.

Jobareth and Lomela, not as much though he'd nothing against them. He certainly liked them well enough to share their Yuletide feast. There was nothing to complain of there; it was nearly as good as one might get back home.

Ah, the back home he had avoided since he became a man. The Cuddon would never have held him, any more than it had his brothers Galaro and Guesare. Maybe this place couldn't have held him either. This place where Guesare had perished, battling Lord Radal. Guesare, at least, had gone back home at last.

Like many another Cuddonian, Habidros would never go back. He knew this. Like many another Cuddonian he would make a new home in a new land.

Now he dozed before the fire blazing in the Great Hall of Castle Rosam. The hearth was impressively massive. It would have held a yule log back home. Back home. There he went again.

Jobareth Nafal drew a chair up beside him. A boy. That's what Nafal was. A boy who had come out here green and lucked through things. He and the countess were both children. But Nafal was making a new home in a new land as surely as he was. He wished him luck.

Aloud, he asked, "So here you are. What next?"

Jobareth smiled at this. "I think the countess and I shall have to figure that out as we go along."

"She'll have to give you some official position, I'd reckon. Something innocuous, like secretary or tutor." He considering adding 'consort to the countess' but held his tongue.

"No. I should have authority from the first or I will not be taken seriously later."

"Maybe so."

"Before leaving Drolwym I suggested Donzalo name me his deputy, to act for him as co-regent. He thought it an excellent idea and put his signature to it."

"Will that go over here?" More than a few of these Lamans might not like a Sharshite holding such a position.

"I think Paren will accept it and his voice is the most important. It would be good if Count Orgelo didn't raise any objections."

"I'll have a word with him," Habidros assured him. He yawned. "And now I'm for my bed," he announced, standing and stretching, before he turned and left the Great Hall of Castle Rosam.

2

Godos barely had time to thank Count Orgelo for his hospitality. Or for the new boots he had gifted him! "Leaving already?" the nobleman asked Galaro. The traders had begun packing up by noon on the day after the Yule.

"The news I've heard here leads me to think I should be elsewhere," answered the trader and the count pursued it no further.

So they crossed the Tod and journeyed away. Galaro seemed in a hurry and no one felt it a good idea to object. "It's probably just as well to get north quickly," said one, "and take our time traveling back south."

Others weren't as sure. "But I thought the plan had been to go slowly up the west side of Weldar and then cross over and go south on the Great Road."

A shrug. "I don't think we'll lose much business and this time I'm willing to give the captain his head."

North they went across the rolling empty country, and then northeast. There seemed to be a road of sorts. Godos knew they should strike the river somewhat north of Todmouth. From there, he could not guess the next move.

~ ~ ~

She did not think an enemy could get to the Silver Plain. It had its wards, just as she did. Radal found it the first time because he was bound up with Donzalo's seeking. The knight's dream had drawn her father here. After that, his connection with Fachalana enabled him to return.

Her father was also connected to Asak. Could that allow the god to reach her? For that matter, could she reach the god and find that part of her Radal said she had lost? Maybe not from here. Maybe she would have to seek outside the protection of the Plain.

She let the silver world fade, returning fully to her room in Drolwym. A small room, grown familiar to her. In one corner, stood the Sword of the Moon. What role was it to play in all this? The fay had believed she would need the sword.

Swords. There was supposed to be another, one the fay had told Blen to seek. He seemed a little skeptical of the whole thing but Fachalana knew better.

She should go find Lady Se. To whom else here might she speak of such things? She was shirking her duty as teacher of Nel and Casurru too.

But the youngsters were elsewhere when she reached Se's chambers. Fachalana knew she did a bad job of it when she tried to explain things to the priestess. Nor, she suspected, did Se truly know much more than she. Less about some things.

But it was good to have someone to talk to, if only to help sort those things out in her own mind. "Were the witches of Nosana linked to Asak too?" she asked. "What I've heard suggests something like that."

Se shook her head. "Most had no powers, save through Nosana. She pulled their familiars to them, linked them so they could manifest and act in this world. As did the hounds drawn by your father from Asak's realm to attack Donzalo. You know that story, don't you? Guesare was with him and told it to us with considerable elaboration."

"I've heard it. Then—what of your own circle?"

"Some are sorceresses, some are not. We work more through our goddess than through magic. But Nosana also worked through a goddess."

"Goddess? I thought she served Asak."

"Nosana was possessed not by Asak but by the Lady of the Dark

Moon, who manifested as a great black cat, to do battle with the silver wolf that Jola called forth and with which she became one."

"Diba."

"Yes, a manifestation of Diba."

"Then who is this Lady of the Dark Moon?"

"A goddess known as Dekata by those who still follow the old Ildin deities, those worshiped before most turned Kamatian. She is vaguely remembered as some sort of demon among the Lamans."

"But she is of the realm of Asak."

"She is of his pantheon, as is Kamat and a rather large number of other gods and godesses. Some say she is Asak's daughter." Se's serious demeanor dropped. "I suspect most Kamatians would be scandalized by that idea! I also suspect Donzalo knows all this from his books. More than I do, quite probably."

"To know is not necessarily to understand."

"That, Lady Fachalana, is very true."

~ ~ ~

Habidros remembered well this inn. He had seen it, a burnt-out shell, when he had ridden north with Sorsen's troop. The work of Radal's mercenary band, under the leadership of his minion Sojel.

Sojel was dead, cut down when he attacked Guesare on the streets of Todmouth, and good riddance to him. He dismounted before the inn. It was early but as good a spot as any to spend the night before riding on. Someone had rebuilt and rebuilt well.

"Ho," he called out on the threshold, "have you a room for a guest?"

"Room a-plenty, sir," replied the woman sweeping the plank floors. She looked familiar, he thought. "Dorbi! See to the gentleman's horse, will you?" The man who emerged from the kitchen, a tall, clean-shaven fellow, seemed a bit familiar too.

And the look he gave Habidros in return suggested he might also find something familiar. The innkeeper had the air of a military man about him. Maybe they had ridden together sometime.

"Certainly, my love. The one night only, sir?"

"Yes, but the one, Master Dorbi." An odd sort of name, that. But Laman ways oft seemed odd to him. "I'll cross Weldar on the morrow."

The man nodded and passed out into the cool air. "It is a while yet till supper, sir," said the woman. Dorbi's wife, presumably. His woman anyway. "I'd be happy to bring you something now, if you wish."

She was young. Youngish—late twenties perhaps. Attractive in a solid fashion, broad-shouldered and broad-hipped. Dorbi didn't look much older.

"Whatever you have on hand would be fine, ma'am. And something to wash it down."

"Right away. You can call me Rassana if you need to call me!" She slipped into the kitchen, where Habidros could see her busying herself through the open doorway.

It was the fourth day after the Yule, now. He had not hurried on his way south.

Dorbi returned to find him with bread and cheese and cold meat and a great flagon of beer. He raised it to the innkeeper. "Dame Rassana tells me you brew this yourself. Fine stuff, sir." He gestured toward an empty chair. "Can you sit a moment?"

Dorbi did, without speaking. "I'm Habidros. Sir Habidros but you needn't worry about the sir part. A Cuddonian."

"That you are," replied Dorbi.

That required a deep laugh and a deep pull on his brew. "I would wager you've been a fighting man yourself at some time." Maybe a sergeant of some troop.

"I once wore sir before my own name. But it was a different name." He leaned back in the chair. "My kid brother and I ran off and joined the Knights of the Flame when we were still lads. Won our spurs with them."

"The Knights of the Flame? Do they still exist?"

"In the north, along the Muram Marches. I'm a northerner myself, as is my wife."

Habidros was entirely willing to accept all this. "A brother, you say?"

"Dead now more 'n a year."

"I lost a brother this past year too," said Habidros, and raised his flagon. "To brothers."

"Aye. To brothers who will never come back." Dorbi rose and returned to the kitchen. Through the open way, Habidros could see him pull Rassana to him and kiss her fiercely.

~ ~ ~

"I am fairly certain Fachalana is a virgin. Not that she has ever said anything to me of it." But there had been plenty enough clues.

Was the priestess surprised? She didn't show it. "Oh, Diba might appreciate that. She is a virgin goddess, you know."

"I did not. We Ani have a huntress deity but she enjoys hunting men too!" A thought came to her. "Is Diba then a patroness of, um, tomboys?"

That brought a laugh. "Hardly. The legend is she lost her true love and will mourn him eternally. When she isn't chasing deer or whatever."

"Oh. Well, I was talking about Fachalana, wasn't I? She never allowed herself a lover back in Sharsh, at least in the time I knew her." Which was, admittedly, not all that long. "She was rather disdainful of all her suitors."

"But not Blen."

"No, not Blen. But she has let herself go only so far with him."

"And he is allowing her."

"Shouldn't he?"

"Oh, I know, no Anian woman would allow herself to be pushed into anything. Maybe it's as well. Our Fachalana still has something to resolve before she can fully commit. She has spoken to me of it."

She would not pry into her friend's confidences. "Someone at her side might be what she needs at this time."

"Again, that may be up to Blen, not her. Only he can convince her he belongs there."

It might be enough just to convince her he belonged in her bed and let things develop as they would from there. Not that she would say that to either one.

But she was becoming mightily impatient with her friends.

3

"With me, Godos, and keep out of the way of those yet to cross." That would take several trips of the ferry and much of the day. He followed Galaro through a village barely large enough to warrant the name, on a dirt path leading up from the landing.

A man approached from the other way, leading his horse. A broad grin broke out when he spied them. "Brother!"

"Habi!" The two rushed forward to envelope each other in bear hugs. They looked much alike. This man was as tall as Galaro, though not so thick, and wore no beard.

The newly-found brother gave the boy a looking over. "This is my, ah, apprentice, Godos. My brother Habidros."

"Sir," Godos greeted him, cautious of the man.

"A Sharshite? Where'd you get this one?"

"Oh, he came off a boat down at the coast." Which was true. "You're heading to County Arvaram, I would wager."

"I was, but I think it can wait another day."

"Do not dawdle too long. I have but come from Tod-ford and your wife-to-be is with child." Galaro winked at Godos. "Unless, of course, that makes you want to turn and run the other way."

To a substantial stone and timber inn they repaired, thatch roofed, with a stable and corrals. "The proprietor here says he hopes to raise horses when he has a bit more money and time to invest. It seems good country for it."

Galaro nodded. "It does. If I ever chose to settle down I'd want a place like this." The moment they entered the big trader exclaimed "Perdos!"

Habidros gave the innkeeper a long looking over. "Sir Perdos. I knew you seemed familiar."

"But I am Dorbi now."

Galaro nodded. If anyone understood such things it was he.

"You were there with us at the taking of Keep Rosam," spoke Habidros.

"That I was and I avenged the death of Count Bolos that night."

"We found the body of their captain on the ramparts. Your doing?"

"It was. We dueled there in the darkness and I had the better of it. Then there was no reason to remain." He sent a fond smile in the direction of Dame Rassana, leaning in the frame of the kitchen doorway. "And I had someone waiting for me."

"I have a whole troop waiting for me. Will you permit my honest traders to camp by your inn tonight, Dorbi?"

"Most certainly, sir, as they once showed hospitality to me."

"Godos, run down and send them this way. I fear this is no place to make any sales but a good one to spend the night. Then on to Ros-town. What are you waiting for?"

The young Sharshite hurried out the doors as the three men sat down to beer and gossip behind him.

~ ~ ~

It was nearly a week after the Yule when Princess Carrana gave birth, but she did give birth. That it was to a healthy girl was seen as a better thing by some than by others. Modareth and Carrana were quite happy with a child of any gender.

"And you're next," said Gawis to his own wife. Before Spring Feast, the doctors assured him. That was less than three months now.

Mara's smile was gentle. "I believe there are many other women in line ahead of me, my husband."

It took him a moment to get the joke. "But none bearing my child." Not this time. He had been faithful to the princess for quite a

111

while. Maybe that was why the gods were finally blessing him with another child.

Or more likely, it was because he had spent more time in his wife's bed. He had fallen in love with her all over again this past year, more than he had ever before. More than any would have ever expected in an arranged marriage to a daughter of the Partanacan emperor.

The stiff dress of golden silk she wore, with its severe vertical lines, largely hid her pregnancy this evening. "Are you sure you are up to the theater? One word and we will cancel."

"And miss the premiere? Sir Pol would be greatly disappointed."

Gawis would not mind disappointing Pol at all. He had mixed feelings about the young man, even if he had saved his brother from an assassin. Twice. "I don't know how he finds the time to write another play."

"Oh, but this one is not his. He is mounting Jobareth Nafal's 'Oemse.'"

"Heard it wasn't ready yet." He was more interested in the man than his play. All sorts of news had come from Lama about Nafal.

"Pol said he—what is the word he used? Oh, yes, polished. He said he polished it for him." There was a tinkle of laughter. "And he resisted all temptation to add his jokes. It is he says a great tragedy."

Those jokes were what made Pol's plays, in Gawis's opinion. He expected a long and tedious evening. But he would be with his wife.

~ ~ ~

Drolwym could be a labyrith to those who did not know it, with its winding halls and winding stairs, its cellars and kitchens and workshops. Blen had explored more of it than his companions here, often finding himself with little else to occupy his time. Maybe he could have, should have, spent that time in the company of Fachalana. She wanted him around, didn't she? But neither seemed willing to say anything of it.

At the moment, he was merely walking those winding hallways, with his thoughts. It was early morn and few were yet stirring. A cat scampered across the hall ahead of him. Drolwym's winding ways were full of cats; one never knew when one might trip over one. The lady Fachalana's room was somewhere up ahead. Maybe he could knock, ask if she wanted to take breakfast with him. He remembered how she once burst into his room at Mountain Keep, with barely a notice of his state of undress, to hasten him off on a mission to speak to the king. Where was that Fachalana now?

Someone stood at her door, seemingly engrossed with its latch. He hid himself around the corner and sneaked another look. Yes, a shape in a dark robe—that's all they were. Nothing more could he tell. They straightened up as the door swung slowly inward. The flash of lamplight on something metal.

Blen leaped forward, sprinting down the hall. "Stop there!" The figure seemed to hesitate, uncertain whether to enter the room or face him. He could see clearly now the dagger in a white hand.

Short. Probably a woman. She slashed at something he couldn't see, something inside the room. Frustration; he was close enough to see that on her face. Close enough to grapple with her.

"Watch out for the blade! It's poisoned!" shouted someone. He barely eluded the sudden swipe of her dagger. Then, looking both ways and seeing no escape, the would-be assassin drove her blade into her own chest and crumpled.

Fachalana. Was she—? She stood unscathed in the doorway, a robe around her. "I dodged her blade too," she whispered. "Who warned you?"

"I did." It was Ansa. She looked at the body on the floor. "I recognized that bluish tinge on its tip at once. My training, you know?"

She gave the pair a slightly sheepish smile. Others were gathering. A sleep-eyed Donzalo appeared behind his wife.

"It is a good thing you are a light sleeper," said Fachalana, "and right across the hall. But I think you'd better go get some clothes on." Ansa was rather scantily clad, in a short shift. She nodded and disappeared into her quarters, her husband following.

"And I've no idea why you were skulking out here," she said, turning to Blen. "But give me a minute and we can go have breakfast." Her door shut.

A guardsman was crouching over the body now. "I recognize her," he said. "Ned's wife. Why would she be up here with a knife?"

That was no question Blen could answer.

~ ~ ~

"Someone threw a rock at me today."

Lomela looked up from her book. An account book? He hadn't realized she personally checked those. "Did they manage to hit you?"

"Not this time."

A distracted nod. "Next time you ride take a guardsman with you." Her attention went back to the figures. Now and again she jotted something down on a paper. He sat and watched for a while.

At last she put her work aside and regarded him, hands steepled below her chin. "Where did you ride?"

"To the embassy. I thought it a good idea to let Lord Doufan in on what I've been doing."

"And what did he think?"

He shrugged. "Who can tell with Doufan?"

"You know him better than most. The bulk of our diplomatic chores are going to fall to you, you know. The next time," she pointed out, "you speak to an ambassador it will be as an official representative of County Rosam."

114

"With an official title?"

A smile. "Deputy Co-Regent is probably all you need. For now."

But not forever. "And what is our future, Lomela? I know it's only four months or so and discretion is necessary—"

She held up a hand to stop him. "I am still in mourning. That is not just show, Jobareth. Bolos was my husband and he died coura-geously. I owe him this."

Lomela had never seemed so like her father. "I understand."

Her smile returned. "Then understand too that the time will come and I will let you know."

4

NED, ONE OF the guardsmen of Drolwym, had no idea of his wife's motives. "She'd been acting odd of late," he claimed. "Off with her friends at all hours and looking the worse for it when she got home. I was thinking maybe she'd taken to drinking."

"We'll have to assume she was mad," the thane told him. "It will be no reflection on you or your children." He reminded himself to gift the man a small amount to help out the family.

But Vantare knew what the dead woman was. Se had made that quite clear—one such as his daughter Nosana, a follower of the darkness. They had not all died.

"An assassin sent by one higher up," she had said. "Or maybe who took it on herself. Certainly not the leader of whatever coven exists now."

"Should we look into those friends Ned mentioned?"

"Not a bad idea," felt his wife. But they found Ned knew no names.

Vantare was a man of moods. He knew this of himself as surely as did those around him. He could find himself listless, disconnected, uncaring of himself and others at times. The thane sometimes blamed himself for how Nosana had turned out. Had his coldness to the child twisted her so? Her mother had died in giving her birth; his sorrow, his loss, always welled up when he saw the girl.

In time, he chose not to look at her at all. He withdrew from all the world, perhaps. Se had helped pull him back when he married her. It might have been too late for Nosana. And the girl hated her stepsister Jola, beautiful, graceful, where she was heavy and homely. The two had been born on the same day.

How many were out there who hated life, who hated themselves, as Nosana had? Was this woman with her knife one such? Vantare had felt that darkness in himself. He understood; in part, at least, he understood.

"We must find where these women meet," he told Se. "They are women, right?"

"I suspect so. Men follow darkness too but we saw only women when the coven attacked Donzalo."

Donzalo and Jola. Vantare thought it had all ended then. He had been wrong.

~ ~ ~

The Great Road was not so great in Godos's estimation. Oh, sure, it was the best road he'd seen on this side of the mountains but it certainly didn't compare with a good many he'd traveled in Sharsh. It *was* paved with stone, at least in places, and there were good bridges that spanned narrow streams rushing down from the hills.

He knew he approached the end of his travels with Galaro and his traders. Ros-town was the place to begin a new journey, back to Sharsh, back to his parents. But it needn't be right away!

The big Cuddonian didn't seem in as much of a hurry now, riding leisurely on. His long talk with his brother had settled him. There was no longer the rush to reach Castle Rosam, where this Guesare had perished. But he was going anyway, to tarry a while, and then trade south, as planned at the start.

"Have you ever traveled on the river, Captain?" Godos asked him. The Weldar was impressive, larger than the Chas or any other river he had seen. Few boats but considerable flotsam dotted its surface.

"Only on ferries from one side to the other. There's not much traffic on it this time of year." Their gazes both went to its flow. "But I've sailed on the sea, as you have. Only trips to Ussan or Lorj and back."

Smuggling. "I may captain a ship some day."

Galaro laughed heartily. "You make it sound like a punishment."

"I like your way of traveling better."

"And you'd be good at it. I can see that, my boy, but I suspect you're meant for a different life."

"Marrying the ugly girl of my parent's choosing and counting what goes in and out of the family warehouses. Which my brother will inherit."

"I do think you may be putting it worse than it really is, but if things don't work out back in Sharsh, we'd welcome you to travel with us again. But bring a stake so you can set up as a proper trader!"

He just might. Still, those theaters and parties in Celatas had their attractions too. He might not want to leave once he was there again.

~ ~ ~

Blen remained vigilant. It gave him something to do and Blen needed something to do. At heart, he was a man of duty. He spied, though he preferred to call it scouting. It was something he was good at. King Lareth had recognized that. 'A man no one notices but who notices everything' the monarch had called him. Sometimes he felt he might notice too much. It could be good to be oblivious.

So it was he had noticed a certain woman who disappeared into the cellars from time to time. He was watching her now.

"What's so interesting?" whispered Nel, crouching beside him. "Something secret?"

He could only nod a yes to that. "Have you been following me?"

"It's possible. You have been acting quite oddly, creeping about like you're invisible or something."

Blen had no good reply to that so he said, "This woman is suspicious."

"What woman?" Drat, she'd disappeared again.

"The suspicious woman I was trailing until you distracted me."

"She had to have gone down those stairs." As she had in the past. "Are you going to follow her?"

"I'd need a torch or lantern."

"She didn't have one."

"She probably knows her way." Blen found himself chuckling. "I can find a lantern and investigate later," he said.

"All right. But I'm going over to take a look right now." The stairs did melt into the dark a few steps down. Nel went down that far and stopped, turning her head slowly as if seeking something. "There is a strange feeling I get here. I'm not sure what it is. Oh, well." She turned and bounded back up to him.

"We are going to explore later," she announced, "but I think I want to talk to Lady Se first. Fachalana, too!"

~ ~ ~

"Letter from Drolwym!" announced Jobareth. He leafed through the dispatches. "Hmm, and from Sharsh and one from Arvaram."

"You open it," ordered Lomela, taking the Drolwym letter.

He perused the short message. "Habi is back and he met his brother Galaro on the road. He's headed here with his traders. Hmm, something about a kid with him we should be interested in. I guess we'll find out about that when he arrives." He put down the piece of paper. "What about yours?"

"Written by Donzalo." That wasn't surprising. "You were right about him and Ansa not waiting. They married a couple weeks ahead of schedule."

"Umm-huh." He was already looking at the messages from Sharsh. From his own family.

"And Fachalana is doing pretty well but still has her ups and downs and she and Blen are still not quite together. You didn't tell me much about that, Jobareth."

119

"I have faith they'll figure it out eventually."

"What's in your letter?"

"Letters. It seems the whole family wrote." He held up a couple pages. "Mother. Father. One of my sisters too."

"But not your fabulously wealthy grandfather?"

"He's more concerned about your father repaying his loans."

"Ooh, that's low of you, Jobareth Nafal."

But common knowledge. It was too bad there were numerous grandchildren to split that fabulous wealth. "Dad's questioning my career choice, as expected, but wishing me success. I'll have to write him about my exalted position here. Hmm, Mom asks about my intentions toward a certain princess. We'll have to get back to her on that."

Lomela had only a "Hmmph" in response to that.

"And my little sister asks if she can come visit."

"She'd be most welcome. As I remember, she is not nearly as obnoxious as you."

It was Jobareth's turn for a "Hmmph."

5

"It was shrewd of the man, that's for certain," allowed Count Orgelo. "I can't see any advantage to opposing this Nafal."

To this his son added, "He's a good lad. I'm proud to have fought beside him."

As Habidros remembered it, Sorsen had arrived when the fighting at Castle Rosam was over. "He is devoted to Countess Lomela," he said. "Jobareth will serve her interests and those of County Rosam, not Sharsh."

Orgelo tossed back his long black hair. "Ha, he may serve them too well! It's good though," he added, giving Habidros an appraising look, "that you have a friendly relationship with him. All the more so with you becoming part of the family. So when do we set a wedding date?"

"I'd wed Lenasha this moment if you got a priest here. Any kind of priest."

"It will have to be a Kamatian priest, boy, and the right kind of Kamatian who recognizes the true Pontifex on Lorj, not that impostor in Oles."

Habidros knew County Rosam did give its allegiance to Oles. It didn't matter at all to him. In fact, he would have asked for a priest of Jov if he'd thought it was possible.

"Too late to call everyone together for a big wedding and feast," the count went on. "Lenasha *is* starting to show. I'd guess you'll be a parent around midsummer."

"Which means it must have happened just before we rode north," said Sorsen.

Lenasha had given him quite a farewell that last night. But it could have been any of several previous nights. "So—tomorrow? Next week?"

"How about this evening? And you'd better go tell her now. It wouldn't do to surprise the girl!"

Surprise? Orgelo and Lenasha had undoubtedly worked it all out already. He was not about to complain; the only thing that needed saying this day was his wedding vows in the big central hall of Orgelo's fortress manor house.

~ ~ ~

"Guesare used to say he felt some place of power near. Perhaps you did as well." Se didn't sound at all convinced of it.

"A place of power? That sounds interesting! What is it?"

Fachalana attempted to answer. "A place where the walls between the worlds are thinner. Not a portal, exactly. One can not pass through it." Where had that knowledge come from? Her head was such a jumble, things her father had told her, things that rose up from his memories, things she had read.

"Where the infinite worlds press more closely. It is said one can see those other worlds more readily in such a place."

Nel nodded solemnly. "Yes. That's what it felt like. Like I could suddenly see a whole bunch of worlds all at the same time!"

"Can you, um, use it for anything?" asked Casurru.

Se glanced at her before attempting an answer. It seemed neither really knew much. "It could make our craft easier. Even for those with less talent."

"Prophets use them," added Fachalana. "Like the Oracle of Cars." The oracle that had set in motion all that happened between her father and Donzalo and the king and herself, prophesying a nebulous danger the lanky Laman posed.

"But whether there truly is a place of power anywhere near Drolwym, I don't know. I've never sensed it," Se told them.

Neither had Fachalana but she thought she might pay more attention now.

"That would sure make our lessons easier," said Casurru.

"You're going to have to do without any help today, young sir," she informed the boy. "Now let me see if your wards are any good."

"They aren't," chirped Nel. "I've been and out of his head a couple times today."

He scowled at the girl, his face reddening.

Se only laughed. "Teenage boys are notorious for letting their attention wander. We'll work on it. And you," she said to the girl, "should know better than do that sort of thing uninvited."

"All right, Lady Se."

Fachalana doubted Nel was the least bit repentant. She might have come down harder on the girl; it was more than just a matter of bad manners. It was a violation, an assault, to enter another that way. She knew from experience.

~ ~ ~

Jobareth was not much older than he was but look at all he had accomplished! Godos examined his own life—short though it was—and saw how much of it had been wasted.

And this Donzalo they talked about. He was even younger than Godos.

Permission had been given Galaro to set up in the empty fair-ground of Ros-town. "Perhaps we'll have to establish a Winter Fair," the countess had jested. Godos liked the woman and was also some-what in awe of the daughter of King Lareth. And she was of about his age too!

It was dreary weather, gray and overcast. The river beside the grounds was the color of lead. A few sluggish shoppers wandered among the tents, whose gay colors and stripes jarred with their surroundings.

"It will pick up," claimed Galaro. "Folks haven't heard we're here yet." But some of his traders were grumbling. Godos had heard them.

Who was that fellow tying his horse up right by the tents? That wasn't permitted, was it? There was a place for that outside the grounds. An old man? Well, maybe not so old. An old soldier, Godos guessed, in buff-coat and breeches, a sword dangling at his side, a wide-brimmed hat shading a forgettable face.

Galaro broke into a broad smile. "Lord Doufan! Welcome!"

Doufan? Yes. He'd seen the man in Celatas, at parties, at court functions, at his own father's house. He was the ambassador here, wasn't he? Godos had forgotten about that.

But of course. Nafal had been his aide or something like that. Legate. That was the title.

"Sir Galaro. Have you any new and interesting gunnes to show me?"

"I might, my lord."

Doufan had turned to him. "And Master Godos Tasetha. I have a letter for you, young sir, from your father." He handed it over without another word, and directed his attention to Galaro's wares.

Godos sat on a bench and examined the missive. The seal remained unbroken. He might have expected Doufan to want to know what was going on. Oh, there had probably been a cover to the ambassador. Godos broke the wax and unfolded the single sheet of heavy paper. The good stuff, and expensive.

My son, it began. Not Godos, as his father usually addressed him.

Congratulations on not drowning. I had considered the sacking of Captain Ferstano but feel more inclined to forgiveness now. Which is a good thing, as he is one of my best men.

Godos had to smile at that, though he knew Fronos Tasetha had intended no jest.

Your mother was overjoyed at hearing from you. Your supposed death hit her hard.

But not Dad? Oh, he wouldn't say, even if it had. He might not even think to say it.

Your letter, short though it was, leads me to assume you are well. As to your companions, I can say only they seem a better sort than you had in Celatas.

That, Godos had to admit, was true.

As to being in County Arvaram, that is another matter, but I am willing to thank Orgelo for sending your letter. As you instructed us to write to the embassy in County Rosam, I assume you did not intend to long stay with him. I shall say you needn't hurry home, now we know you live. Winter is not the best time to travel and there are opportunities to learn everywhere. That, after all, is why we sent you abroad.

One reason.

But do write so your mother and I know where you are, and let us know when you intend to return so we may prepare your homecoming.

Line up a bride, most likely. It was signed simply with his father's name. He looked up to see Galaro and the ambassador huddled over a book. He hadn't known the trader carried that sort of merchandise. Ah, when he walked over he could see a tiny wheel-lock pistol concealed within it.

"Most useful for an assassin, wouldn't you think?" asked Doufan.

"Maybe if his target were in a library, sir."

"Ha, quite so. If I ever need to shoot Sir Donzalo I'll keep that in mind."

Galaro chuckled at that. The jest meant nothing to Godos. "But a gunne that size could be useful anyway," he ventured.

"So it could, lad, and so I, ah, may purchase it if this fellow will give me an honest deal." Galaro might have smirked just a little. "When you have a reply to that, bring it by the embassy and I'll send it along to Sharsh. Or carry it myself; I don't know day to day whether I'm going to be here or there."

"Thank you, my lord."

"And when Galaro returns south in a few days, you may come and stay with us."

"The countess invited him to stay at the keep," Galaro informed him.

"Just as good. Thirty Royals, you say? Robbery, man. Robbery!"

~ ~ ~

He knew the stairs Nel had described. He'd always heard they were unused, that they went nowhere except to a spot where the roof had collapsed, so long ago that no one was sure just when.

Casurru lit his candle and started down. He certainly didn't feel anything. Maybe it had just been the girl's imagination. The little flame flickered, revealing walls cut from the rock on which Drolwym Castle was built.

And some thirty-two steps down—the boy had counted—there was a jumble of fallen rock. He could go no further.

But—was there something? It was like faint distant voices. Whispers in the darkness. For a moment, Casurru felt like bolting back up the steps. No, no. He would see this through. There probably wasn't really any 'place of power.' And he couldn't get at it if there was. Slowly, the boy began to climb upward again.

Why did his candle flicker so right here? The flame danced on its wick, pulled toward his right. He felt along the wall. There was a shallow alcove there. He'd noticed that before. Just more rock at its back. But that draft came from somewhere. He held the candle high and examined the wall. Nothing. Casurru was disappointed, and ready to continue upward.

"Damn!" He could curse here where his elders wouldn't admonish him. "Damn," he said again, liking the sound of it. Wait. To his left, a narrow opening between the rocks, an opening that would be near impossible to see from the stairs.

Not so narrow maybe. It was easy to squeeze through. Another stairway lay a few paces ahead, leading quite a different direction from the one he had just left. He could go back and tell someone what he had found. Or he could go down it a little way and look around. That wouldn't hurt anything, would it?

Down and down he went, stairs here, tunnel there, but there was only one way so he wasn't afraid of getting lost. Well, maybe he was a little afraid. Then the walls were no longer close about him. Casurru sensed he was in a large cave of some sort. He essayed a whistle and heard it echo from distant walls. It was hard to see much by the illumination of one little candle as he stepped further into the cavern.

A sudden gust of wind took that light away.

6

"I GOT A peek at the new royal child. She looks much better than either of her parents!"

"Give her time," replied Erlana Nafal. She was a bit miffed that she hadn't been invited to the baby's naming ceremony. Now her sister-in-law was bragging about being there. That made it worse.

"I wonder if she'll be skinny like her father, or—" Simesa hesitated to use the word that was surely on the end of her tongue.

"Fat," Erlana supplied. Princess Carrana was fat.

"Stout might be better."

She could only shrug. Carrana reputedly didn't care and she couldn't hear them anyway. "I wish Jobareth would write," she said. She needed a change of subject.

"County Rosam is a very long way from Celatas," her mother reminded her.

Erlana knew that. The king's own fleet couriers took weeks, even with frequent changes of mount. Jobareth had told her so. It sometimes seemed like he was the only one who ever told her anything interesting. Her other brothers talked about wine.

And now it seemed he was going to stay in that distant place on the far side of Lama. She wished he'd stayed home and married Fachalana. Even if her father had disgraced himself or died or something. The different rumors did not agree on things.

She'd ask Jobareth. He knew all about it. Anyway, she liked Fachalana.

"Your brother is likely to show up here one of these days with another book's worth of dreary poems to print," predicted Simesa.

"I like his poems!"

"So do I, dear," spoke her mother, "though I don't understand most of them."

"Maybe I'll be a poet too," Erlana claimed.

Simesa might have smirked. "Oh? Let's hear something."

Now she was on the spot! "All right," she said, sitting up straight and reciting as she might have for her governess when small.

The carpenter bee a carpenter be
When she drills holes in a tree;
No harm in this can I see
So long as she drill none in me!

"Better than Jobareth's," felt her sister-in-law and they moved on to other topics.

~ ~ ~

"Fachalana!" Nel came running to her. "It's Casurru, He's in trouble." She frowned. "He tried to call you but you blocked him out."

It took but a second to digest that. "Take me to where you speak."

It was not hard to follow the girl. She knew exactly where she was going. Maybe this pair had been practicing speaking from afar on their own.

Casurru?

Hi Fachalana. I'm lost.

Lost? Where?

Under the keep somewhere. I followed a passage down to a big cave and then I lost my light and I can't find the way back up again.

She would tell the boy what an idiot he was later. He sounded scared right now though he was doing his best to hide it. *We'll come for you. Don't move! And I'll remain open if you call again.*

"We need Sir Blen," she told Nel.

"And lanterns!"

"Yes, and lanterns."

She was only slightly surprised to find Blen already had lanterns. "I went down that stairway yesterday but I couldn't find any way through."

A few minutes later they were gathered at the top of the stairs. To Nel, she said, "I want you to stay right here so you can relay messages if I call you from afar."

"Can I keep talking to Casurru?"

"Absolutely." It might help keep the boy calm.

She called him herself right then. *Where is the way? Blen couldn't find one.*

Fachalana had no difficulty locating the hidden passage Casurru described. Blen might have sworn softly as he followed her.

As they wound downward, he whispered—one felt it necessary to whisper here—"I see you wear your sword."

"As do you." She had indeed buckled on the Sword of the Moon. She felt more secure going into the unknown with it at her hip. Maybe Blen was the same.

A place of power. There *was* a place of power here. She could feel it with every step downward she took. Maybe that was why Casurru had spoken effortlessly to her. There was less resistance to sending himself elsewhere.

Fachalana reached out to the boy. Ah, he was chatting with Nel. She wouldn't intrude. She was his cousin, right? Casurru was the son of Vantare's sister and Nel was the thane's granddaughter. Once removed or something like that. Then the walls around them disappeared, their lanterns now an island of light in a great darkness, enclosed by unseen walls.

"Hey! I can see you!" cried out Casurru.

"Come to us," Blen called back. "Best we not get too far from that passageway either," he said in a lower voice.

It shouldn't matter with their lanterns. They should be able to find their way around and Fachalana had an urge to explore. Oh, maybe it would be better to wait on that.

There was the boy, trying to look composed.

Then Blen pitched forward and many arms grabbed at her, many bodies smothered her, bore her to the hard, cold floor, and all was dark.

~ ~ ~

"The boy is torn," said Lomela. "Part of him wants to be on the road again with Galaro." Young Tasetha was dawdling in the court-yard below, watching men and women come and go. The Cuddonian trader had just ridden away.

"I don't blame him one bit. Maybe I'll run off myself some night."

"No one's stopping you." That would shut him up. "You know his family."

"I do," replied Jobareth. "I knew Godos for that matter. He seemed the worst sort of wastrel in Celatas."

"His family is respected. And nearly as wealthy as yours."

"True. Our families are not exactly rivals, not being in quite the same businesses. But both are involved with shipping things from one place to another."

"I rarely saw the Tasethas at court. You Nafals seemed to think yourselves part of the royal family."

"Mostly none but me, my lady. And my grandfather, keeping an eye on his investments." She gave him a warning glare. "But it was indeed mostly me and I am forever grateful to your father for allowing me to be companion to you and Modareth when we were small."

"And Fachalana. Don't forget Fachalana."

"Our ringleader in mischief." Both smiled at the memory. They had fallen in love then, while still children. "Godos was a part of your brother's circle."

"Gawis. Godos was never very close to him. That circle has largely melted away, my father tells me, and Gawis has become serious about his duties."

"As apparently has Godos. His father did well to send him to sea, even if it didn't go quite as planned!"

Lomela laughed. "It was more complicated than that! I thought you knew more of what was involved."

"Oh? I don't get personal letters from the king, you know."

"More of the story came from Fachalana. You remember she fought an assassin at Modareth's house."

"I remember the tale. That's why the king named her a viscountess."

"And fixed a handsome income on her as well. You missed out by not marrying the girl! The thing is, the would-be assassin had ties to Godos. No one believed he was involved but his father thought it prudent to get him out of Sharsh and my father agreed. Or maybe more than just agreed."

"Ties?"

"Oh, I understand he was the sort of man to do a bit of rough work for young blades like Godos."

Jobareth nodded. "I've known toughs like that, who attach themselves to moneyed lads."

"Not yourself, of course." No, she shouldn't have said that.

But Jobareth considered the statement seriously. "Had someone fixed an allowance on me like Godos had, who can say? But I was busy studying at the university and only caroused now and again."

"No, Jobareth. All the money in the world wouldn't have changed you from—from the boy I loved. And the man I love."

Then Lomela came to his arms. She was letting him know it was time.

7

TRAPPED AND BOUND! Robed and hooded figures ringed about them, holding torches. Hmm, not so many. A dozen? Two great braziers lit up the area around them.

Where were the others? Fachalana and Casurru were trussed up as he was. They probably hadn't been clouted over the head first, though.

That one was surely their leader. She looked no different, stood no taller, but she moved as one with authority. The woman pulled back her hood and looked them over. "I am Vis," she stated.

Casurru squinted at her. "I know you. You work at Mausare's farm."

"All of our coven are your neighbors, humble wives and servants. But we are much more!" There was a murmur of agreement. What were those bowls the women were passing back and forth? "Now you know us and you know our secret cave. You can not be permitted to leave."

"Do you think that is up to you?" came Fachalana's voice, imperious, dismissive of this woman's proclamation.

"I do, my lady. We have the upper hand this time, not as when our coven faced your sister. Not all of us were there on that night. Some remained in this place, to lend its power to Nosana. Now others have joined us. Now we rebuild."

"This is a place of power," said Fachalana. "And you have power, don't you? In some little part." Blen saw Vis's face contort. "I have more."

The viscountess was acting, Blen suddenly realized, as surely as she would have on the stage in Celatas. Even hamming it up, not that he would ever tell her so!

The leader of the coven stood staring at her for quite some time. "Then perhaps you should join us. You could lead and—and yes, I would follow you. I would, as Nosana once followed your father."

Fachalana's scorn was evident. "Radal used her for his own ends and let her perish when she was of no use."

That did not have the effect she had apparently expected. "Yes, yes. He let her serve and then pass into the great darkness! We would too, my lady."

Fachalana did not seem to know what to say next.

"When Nosana was no more than a child," began Vis, "she found this place. Here she heard the voices of the Lady of the Dark Moon and of great Asak himself. This place—" Her arms swept wide. "This place is indeed a place of power. It aided Nosana in discovering her own powers. It opened her to Asak."

"Or to someone," said Fachalana. "But never mind that. It all came to the same end. Incidentally, I have spoken from afar and others are on their way down here. This cavern will never be your secret again."

The women howled. Drugged, thought Blen, as he surveyed their crazed faces. He struggled against the ropes restraining him. No good.

But Fachalana rose and her bonds dropped from her. "Don't you know you can't tie up a powerful sorcerer, woman? I need but reach around through another world and undo your knots."

The coven shrank from her but Vis stood steady. A pale, sickly-green light began to play about her form.

Fachalana laughed. "You will fight?" Above her, a golden nimbus formed and began to shape itself into a great eagle. Vis looked at it a moment and her lights faded. She turned and ran into the dark.

"No match and she knew it!" But not so her acolytes. They ringed her around, their hands as claws, ready to rush upon her, to tear her apart. There was no magic here, only drugged madness.

"Your sword," cried out Blen. It lay forgotten on the floor. Both did. If only he could get hold of his!

"Good idea." She swept the Sword of the Moon from the floor and from its scabbard in one motion, as the women charged. Two dropped. Others bled, but he was not certain they felt their wounds. They backed away, confused and in disarray, to again circle her, shrieking and screaming, but their resolve was broken. One after another fled gibbering away, leaving them alone.

~ ~ ~

"It is better to look to ones next step than all those that led to it."

"The ambassador is full of sayings like that," Jobareth told him. "You'll have to come to expect them."

Doufan shook his head. "This boy showed me much more respect when I was his superior."

"It's good advice anyway, sir," said Godos. He grinned. "I should learn some to have on hand too."

"They work better when you seem old and wise," said Jobareth.

"Or simply old," added the ambassador. "Here's the place."

'The place' was a low-roofed restaurant by the wharves, frequented by boatmen and stevedores. On the wharves, in part. "It is likely to be the last time I visit here." Doufan sounded wistful. "Or visit Lama at all. I think my days of foreign postings end with this one, lads."

"You'll retire, sir?" asked Godos.

Jobareth almost snickered at the idea. "It is more likely the king will put you in charge of something in Celatas, isn't it?"

"Lareth has hinted something of the sort. I might be asked to sit on his council." He shook his head. "And I might turn it down."

But probably not. "What do you recommend for our lunch, um, Old Dog?"

Godos looked from the one to the other and mouthed, "Old Dog?"

"An alias I used when I roamed Ros-town. There's perhaps no point anymore. The catfish is good. Or the fowl, fried with batter in true Laman style."

"That means greasy and spicy," Jobareth informed the young man.

"I'll have both! I had a good meal at an inn down south. Dorbi's Crossing. Galaro and Habidros both knew the owner."

"Our old friend Perdos. I've kept track of him," said Doufan. "We'll order now, mistress. Catfish for me and fried fowl for this gentleman, right?" Jobareth nodded. "And the young fellow across the table wants both. Plenty of fried dumplings."

"Yes, sir. We haven't seen you in a while, Grandfather Dog," she said.

"Sadly true. And it may well be the last time I'm here. Run along now and fetch us our meal."

When she was gone, Jobareth whispered, "Perdos?"

"Aye. He did some scouting for me in our troubled times. He was there at the castle too, that last night. I think he'd made his peace with Sir Guesare before the end."

Nafal wondered how much else he was ignorant of. "I'm afraid our own network of spies is now nonexistent."

"Our?"

Jobareth felt himself blush. "County Rosam's."

"The men who served are still about. You can rebuild it. But don't make the mistake of the late count and have both personal spies and an official service. They got in each others way and confused Bolos with conflicting reports."

Godos smirked. "But someone has to spy on the spies!"

"They can do that quite well themselves. Ah, here's our lunch. The steaming platters were placed before them on a dark wooden table soaked with the grease of thousands of such meals, and their conversation turned to more ordinary things.

~ ~ ~

The thane himself burst into the circles of light cast by the braziers, a handful of doughty Cuddonian guardsman at his heels. Nel followed at a discreet distance.

"Fachalana," she yelled out and ran to her. The woman was sitting, hunched over, on the floor, seemingly dazed. "What's wrong with her?"

"Her battle took a lot out of her. Sorcery is hard work, I've learned," reported Blen. "She should be up in the keep and in her bed."

"We'll have to get her up those narrow stairs," began Vantare.

"No need. Casurru scouted around and found another entry."

"Over that way." The boy pointed. "It makes sense all those women wouldn't come through the castle."

"Women." The thane looked at the two bodies on the floor. "I know one of these."

"Some of the others too, sir," said Casurru. "I recognized a bunch of them."

"Are they all sorceresses?" wondered Nel.

"I don't think so," the boy replied. "Maybe a couple. Or maybe only their leader."

Two men made a chair of their arms for Fachalana and all followed Casurru into a tunnel on the far side of the cavern. They emerged in an old stone building, small and falling into ruin.

"A temple of those who dwelt here before us," murmured Vantare. "Most avoid them."

"Before us?" Nel had never heard such a thing before.

"A dark people. Maybe related to those of the Muram Marches or the upper Siph. They left these places here and there. The standing stones where the Lady Se holds the rites of Rema is one."

"Oh. I'm going to be a priestess of Rema."

"Remember there are other goddesses, child. Gods too, for that matter."

"Diba needs followers," came Fachalana's voice, not very loud. "She told me so herself. How far to home?"

"Just up the hill here. Let's go, lads"

Nel tried to sit and watch by Fachalana after they put her to bed, but fell asleep in time. She dreamed that she had become a priestess of Diba the Huntress, and carried a silver bow like the goddess, with a shaggy wolf at her heels. It was a pretty good dream.

8

"Brother Grippo. It is good to see you with us again."

"Your grace. I felt it time to resume my robes."

"Indeed, indeed," said the hierophant. "But taking a year off doesn't seem to have hurt you any. Perhaps all novices should before taking their vows."

"It seemed a good idea at the time." What with a new count who disliked and then dismissed his brother, and all the turmoil about Castle Rosam. Around County Rosam.

"And it probably was, my boy." The high priest was a short, balding innocuous-looking man of middle years, who had put on a little too much weight. Grippo knew he was also a politician at heart; one didn't rise to his position without it. "But there is no reason for you to be hanging about the seminary. You completed all your training long ago!"

Grippo could only shrug. "Where else should I be, your grace? My family is distant, at Sir Paren's keep, and I can't continue taking advantage of the hospitality of the countess."

"You probably could, and you know it. Countess Lomela is fond of you. Here, sit." Both settled on a stone bench. They caught the full sun there; pleasant on a winter day. "I could assign you as chaplain when you are a priest."

That would create some ill will among his brethren, he was sure. "You know the ways of the powerful, Brother. Many of those who will stand beside you this midsummer are of peasant families, men we will disperse to villages and never again hear much of."

"I would not mind spending time in a village." Not at all. Getting away from intrigue sounded desirable.

"Oh no, we won't let you hide away! And I won't let you hide here, right now. Get your things together; you're going to come serve in my house." That statement was followed by a friendly smile. "I could use a good secretary."

Pretty much the capacity in which he had been serving Jobareth Nafal for some months, first at the embassy, then the keep. The hierophant would be fully aware of that. "As you will, your grace."

There were far worse ways to fill the five months until his ordination. If he didn't bolt before then. Grippo was still unsure of his vocation, of his future.

And the hierophant's house in Ros-town was warm and comfortable, quite unlike this pile of stones in the hills.

~ ~ ~

"I'd bet just having the Sword of the Moon in your hand would have been enough to make Vis run."

She wouldn't have needed to call on her power and exhaust herself. Fachalana knew what Blen was implying. She also slightly resented this mild reproof. "She vanished into the darkness. I wonder where she went."

"No rumor of her. They've tracked down some of the coven. One had died from a wound you gave her. A couple others killed themselves and some ran off. The thane hasn't decided what to do with the three we do have in custody."

"Not execution?" The women were more deluded than they were evil. And what harm had any of them actually done?

"No, that he ruled out. Maybe they need to go and dream in the caves of the fay!"

"If only it were so simple. Their sickness is not the sort that can be healed on the Plain of Silver." And, in its way, perhaps more difficult to cure.

Blen nodded. "Lonely and unhappy, drawn in when they found a community."

"You understand." Better than she, maybe. "The drugs may have had something to do with it as well. I feel like getting out of bed now."

He might not have approved but he did not object. "Do you need any assistance dressing?"

"Not from you, sir!" Blen reddened at once.

"I meant Ansa," he mumbled. "Oh, you're joking." Shaking his head, he exited her room. Maybe she shouldn't have laughed so much.

And maybe she wouldn't mind his assistance so much, dressing or even undressing. That was a thought for another time! She slipped from the covers. Oh, that floor was cold, even through the thick wool rug. What to wear? Only three dresses had come north with her from County Rosam and she was tired of them. The brown one.

She must find a seamstress here and have something new made. At least one dress! Who knew how long it would be till they left Drolwym? But leave they would, leave this comfortable, ramshackle keep, and face the world again.

First, she must face herself, here in this place. Or in the place of power that lay far beneath it. It was there she could reach out into the worlds, *would* reach out and seek that part of her still missing.

Now for some breakfast.

~ ~ ~

Jobareth Nafal put pen to paper. He missed having his secretary at hand. Madin was not the same and Lomela kept him busy.

A rap on the frame of his open door. "Lord Doufan is here, sir," said a maid. "He would like a word with you."

"Thank you, mistress." What was her name? He should know the staff better. "Send the ambassador in."

Doufan entered, dropped into a chair, and at once announced, "Word has come a new ambassador is on his way. Besvanis Nesic."

Jobareth knew him—a lackluster career diplomat, a man who would never have been able to handle the events of this past year. "You will be leaving when he arrives?"

"I'll move into our house in town while Nesic is learning what he needs. Or what he can. There's no one else left to show him." The sigh was deliberately dramatic. "Unless, of course, you came back to the embassy."

That was but a passing jest. Both knew it would not happen. "I am charged still to deliver Lady Fachalana to Celatas. Not until then will I leave," continued Doufan. "Who can guess when that will be?" He glanced at the papers on Jobareth's desk. "Official correspondence?"

"Letters to my family."

"You will have to exert some official authority eventually."

"Best I take my time, I think. It will be easier when I marry Lomela. She has accepted my proposal."

"Congratulations, my boy. I knew it would happen eventually. But you'll not be rushing to a wedding, I would think."

"We might announce it in the fall." A year after the death of Bolos. That was long enough.

Doufan nodded. "And perhaps a Yuletide wedding? I must insist Lareth send me as his representative at the ceremony."

"You would be welcome in whatever capacity you came, sir."

"I thank you." Then, in more serious tones, "Let us hope County Rosam approves too."

"I seem to be liked well enough here in the keep."

"Because they know you. The rest of the county does not. You should be seen more. Not doing anything in the name of the countess, just riding out and meeting the people. Brother Grippo might be able to help you with that, if the hierophant will lend him now and again. Everyone likes Grippo."

"It wouldn't hurt to be more friendly with the hierophant for that matter." He had been meaning to visit him.

"Indeed not, though he's not as well-liked as Grippo! Give my greetings to your family, sir," he said, rising. "Now I must pay my compliments to the countess. But not my congratulations, I think. Best she not know I'm in on the secret."

"I trust in your discretion, Lord Doufan."

Though he had no doubt, as the man left his little office, that he would write of this news to the king. That mattered not at all.

Jobareth Nafal again took up his pen.

~ ~ ~

"I was able to call up my abilities as never before. Well, no. When I drew upon the Sword of the Moon, the sword that remains in the Temple of the Dawn, the—" She decided not to say Firebird. "Whatever is in me came out in all its power."

"Perhaps not *all* its power. That might well be immeasurable." The elf let her think about that a few moments before saying, "You realize you are more than just a sorcerer, don't you?"

Donzalo's words about divine ancestors returned to her. "I don't know what I am, Arsel."

The pair sat on the bench before Jola's cottage. She had come there to think. It was likely the fay had done the same.

"An excellent sorcerer," he replied. "More than excellent. But, as a human, no more than that. Others have been more gifted, your sister included." He might have given the slightest of shrugs. "And your father."

"As a human." It was not a question. She knew what Prince Arsel

144

implied. "It is as a human I must search for what I have lost in the realm of Asak."

"I think so. Your other nature is separate from that."

Yes, of course it was. She recognized the truth of it. "Then I must return to that place of power and seek. I do not think I could succeed elsewhere."

"There are other such places that should do as well. Places near your own home in Sharsh." His pale indigo eyes turned westward. "The place you knew as the Cave of Ghosts as a child."

"Really? The maids at our house would tell me the scariest stories of it!" Which she loved. She would have to visit when she returned. "But I think I need do this here and now."

"Only you can make that choice."

And it had already been made.

9

"Do you ride to the hounds, Jobareth?" asked Godos. "I'm told Count Borrago was a great one for the chase."

"Not I," admitted Nafal. "There is still a kennel of his hunters. Master Saj takes them out for exercise now and again."

"Nor I," Godos said. "It seems the thing to do when one is a country gentleman." His own father had given it a try but found himself with a complete lack of interest.

"I'm hardly a country gentleman! But I do enjoy riding across this countryside."

As did he. It was a rolling landscape, neatly laid out in pasture and farm field with the occasional hedge row, and not so far from Castle Rosam. A bit northwest, he thought, somewhere above the town.

The third rider spoke. "There's little to chase anymore. The last wolf seen in these parts was pulled down the day after you arrived here, Jobareth. For Ros's naming day."

"Yes, Grippo. I heard about it at the time. Coyotes still roam, and foxes. There are always foxes."

Neither would be likely to mention the man with whom Jobareth had arrived; by now Godos had heard most of the stories of Lord Radal and Donzalo Rosam and all the rest.

"There's a hamlet over that way." Grippo pointed. "We could ride through and let you smile at everyone."

"Ha, and maybe throw handfuls of coins to them?"

"That would seem a bit too extravagant, but the occasional copper to a child might go over. Hmm." Grippo thought no more than a few seconds. "Maybe not until after you're married, so your largess is connected to the countess."

"Married?" This was the first Godos had heard of it.

"Who, me? I don't know anything about anyone getting married!" Still seemingly jesting, Jobareth added, "And neither do you."

"I understand." Quite well he understood. No one was going to accuse Godos Tasetha of being dense! "Of course, that means you'll see no wedding gift from me."

"I do suspect I'll have to be sending you one first. Your parents are sure to have someone all ready to go before a priest with you."

"Oof. Don't remind me of those sorts of things, Jobareth Nafal. I'm still free now." He looked across the fields. "And maybe I'll decide to stay that way. Say, Grippo, would there be wine at that hamlet?"

"There's only one way to find out." The young acolyte spurred his steed forward. His friends followed.

~ ~ ~

Fachalana did not intend to hurry. She needed her strength. The cavern remained, ready when she was ready.

Today, she visited it with Se and some of her priestesses. "I feel the power now," admitted Se. "Maybe I always did, just a little, and ignored it."

With torches, they went all about the space, measuring its extent, looking for other ways in and out. Yes, Vantare's men had already surveyed it thoroughly. The thane was understandably nervous about this unknown cave hidden beneath his keep. They had discovered no other ways than the two already known, though there seemed to be a draft from somewhere above.

One of the priestesses came across a discarded bowl, sniffed at the bit of liquid still in its bottom, wrinkled her nose. "I don't recog-nize it," she told Se. Se sniffed and shook her head too.

Fachalana didn't even attempt to identify it. She knew nothing of such things, though she had learned of certain restorative elixirs from her father. "If anyone would know what it is, I'd bet on Ansa," she said. "Or her brother, were he around."

Se tossed the bowl aside. "It does not matter."

The two tall bronze braziers still stood, now cold. Firewood or charcoal would need be brought in here were they ever to used again. That would be a lot of trouble. Maybe the coven had only lit them now and then.

And she couldn't see those women carrying the heavy stands into the cavern. Might they have already been here when Nosana first found it? Had some others used it in an immemorial past? Maybe that folk who had built the temple, who had lived here before the Krevi.

There was a sort of altar. Or maybe it was intended as a podium. The rest of the place was empty. "One could sure store plenty of turnips down here," remarked Fausala.

"Pah," said one of her companions. "Wine!"

"Great place to brew beer!" rose another voice.

"But not a good place," decided Se, "for those of us with talents to linger overlong. Let's go up the stairs instead of traipsing back through that temple. And," she promised, "there *is* wine in the keep."

There were sounds of approval. Fachalana decided she should say something before they started moving. "This—this place of power should be off limits to those who might be endangered by it. Children especially. I wouldn't want Nel or Casurru or any other gifted youngster getting into trouble down here."

"Verily so," agreed Se. "I'll tell Vantare to put a guard on both ways in, if he hasn't already."

Maybe no one should get in without permission, Fachalana told herself as she followed the women into the passage. No one but her.

~ ~ ~

"A letter from Jobo? Is there anything to me?" wondered Erlana.

"Not specifically, my dear," said her mother. "It's really rather brief." There was a bit of a knowing smile. "And though he doesn't actually say it, it seems he and the princess are getting along well."

Mother would always refer to Lomela as 'the princess,' though she was a countess now. And Erlana wasn't at all surprised the two of them were together. At last!

"He has befriended young Godos Tasetha, who showed up there somehow, and commends him to us. He says he's promised to visit when he returns to Sharsh."

"Godos? He was a horrible boy!"

"He was, wasn't he? Your brother claims he has turned into a decent man."

"Jobo is far too trusting," Erlana declared.

"That's better than being mistrustful of everyone."

"I suppose." She wasn't completely convinced of it. "I'd still like to go visit him."

"Who knows what the future might hold, my dear?"

Nothing fun, the girl feared. Nothing fun at all.

~ ~ ~

"Are we all going to travel together when we go?" asked Blen. He assumed they would go someday. "I know our destinations are not the same. Not in the end."

"Or for that matter, what route will we take?" Ansa added to this. "The way we came or down the Great Road?"

Donzalo looked from one to the other. At least Fachalana wasn't pestering him; she sat a bit aside, looking a little too amused. "The way up through the Cuddon made sense in late fall, especially with a wagon," he said. "We could have taken the Road but there would have been too many questions and too many delays and we would have needed to go roundabout with it in the north to reach Drolwym."

"We're not taking the wagon back? It belongs to Lomela, you know," Ansa reminded him.

"And Fachalana's had new dresses made. There will be much baggage."

That annoyed the viscountess. "We can leave them," she declared. "I intend to ride and ride fast."

Blen had hoped to hear this. "Then the Great Road. But that won't take you and Ansa to your home."

"Nor will it take you," Donzalo reminded him. "You could go straight across the King's Road through Oles and on to Sharsh."

Fachalana was even more annoyed by that. "We are going to County Rosam. There is no way we leave Lama without first seeing Lomela."

"Then we should all travel there together. It's not so far out of the way for us."

"How far?" asked Fachalana. "Are you going to be able to visit Castle Rosam sometimes?"

"Four days from there up to my uncle's place. Then another three or so, traveling at a normal pace. We could knock a day off that, maybe, if we took a more direct route."

Ansa added, "And we could always hurry a bit."

"Oh, certainly. I, um, hope you won't be too disappointed by the place."

"I think I know what to expect of Felewym, Laird Donzalo. I've seen the area, you know, when I visited the Anian house there."

"The inn where your brother meets his fellow spies? I'm not certain I like being so close to it."

"It's as safe as anywhere in the Cuddon."

"Hardly a recommendation! But yes, Fachalana, we can visit my birthplace without too much traveling."

"Less than me," she murmured, apparently to herself.

"We are going to visit them sometimes too," Blen asserted. And, yes he had said 'we.' Let her make of it what she would.

"Very well. But there is business first to finish here."

10

Ambassador Nesic duly arrived, with entourage, and Doufan prepared to move from the embassy. "Why don't you come stay in the house with me?" he asked Godos. "We can enjoy the town a while."

A few hours later, they sat their horses before the modest two-story building, Godos looking it up and down. "And no one else stays here?"

"Not now. It was useful once." A place where diplomats could stay overnight in town, or unofficial guests of the embassy. Fachalana and Ansa had stayed there a while. Sir Guesare too. And more recently, there was Doufan's occasional tryst with his mistress. That was over and it was just as well. "My secretary will come down and join us on the morrow. Busy packing things up now. There is a stable right up the street where we can keep our mounts."

As they walked back from it, he pointed out a few places of interest. "That food stall used to be good. The woman who ran it was Rassana, whom you met far from here. Not so good now. There's a spring house up this street here." He gestured to their left. "Jobareth kept some wine there. Chilled wine is most welcome in a Laman summer! I suspect it is all gone now."

"His family could send him more," Godos pointed out.

"And send it to the castle, alas. Here we are." An erect, middle-aged man opened the door to them. "Sergeant Ubos, retired," said Doufan. "Our butler now."

And bodyguard, if need be. He expected need not to be; things were peaceful in Ros-town, in County Rosam, and likely to remain that way.

"Some supper, sir?" asked Ubos. The old soldier pretty much looked through his young companion. He'd warm to the boy or if he didn't they'd be gone soon enough. Both of them. He should arrange something for Ubos. That idiot Besvanis was entirely likely to dismiss him. In fact—

"Would you like to come to Sharsh, Sergeant? I could use a steady fellow like you."

"Thank you, sir, but no. I've bought me a little plot upcountry and am planning to retire to it when you go."

"Good then. I'm glad to see you were thinking further ahead than me, Ubos."

The man grinned. "There's been a lot of free time to think recently." He went off to prepare a meal.

"I never paid much attention to servants before," admitted Godos. "I have learned things in Lama that I should have known long ago."

"Some people never learn them, Master Tasetha. It only took nearly drowning for you."

They settled at a round oak table. He poured out a little red wine for each of them, the cheap and not very flavorful—but potent—wine of the south.

"Have you considered the diplomatic service, lad? I think you might have a flair for it."

"It's a lot like selling things, isn't it? Except you don't make as much profit!" The boy laughed at his joke.

"No, I'm afraid we don't even get offered many bribes."

"Probably not for me," said Godos, becoming more serious. "Not that I have much interest in the family business either. Hey, something smells good!"

"Ubos is a fine cook. One reason I offered him a job."

"Praise a bridge when it is crossed and a meal when it is eaten," stated Godos, who then snickered. "I've been learning some of those aphorisms you like."

"Don't be surprised if I appropriate it."

"I'd be disappointed if you didn't, sir."

Lord Doufan raised his glass in salute to that.

~ ~ ~

The guard only nodded to her at the head of the stairs. He had no orders to stay Lady Fachalana. Down she went, turning into the side tunnel, descending toward the cavern.

Maybe she should have said something to someone. Ansa or Se. Not that there would be any point. It was possible Se or some other would sense what she was up to when she sent herself out into the other worlds.

That was a matter of her using a place of power close to them. In truth, any wizard, anywhere, might sense her if she did not ward properly. That fellow from Partanaca. Axacles. She was certain he posed no threat. But there were more potent wielders of sorcery. Perhaps more potent than she, or at least more practiced.

Fachalana spread the carpet she had carried rolled up under her arm. If she was going to sit here a while it wasn't going to be on that cold rock! Now where?

Radal had been enmeshed with Asak and she had been enmeshed with Radal. But not bound; so her father had told her. She might as well think of the apparition as her father, though it was not quite. A part of him, disconnected from the Radal that had been.

And a part of her had been pulled along with him. Lost. That's what it was. She needed to find it, restore it. She needed to seek Radal first, wherever he was.

Fachalana sought through the worlds.

~ ~ ~

In his house in the far southern isles, Axacles felt a disruption in the worlds. Someone reaching out—to where?

To a world of the gods. That was dangerous. A fleeting smile. Dangerous was hardly the word. The daughter of Radal. That's who it was. Curiosity contended with caution. Dare he follow her a little way? Safer than exploring on his own but still—not safe.

I see you, came her voice.

I intend no harm.

Do not get in my way.

He would not. He closed himself, threw up every ward he could to shut out what was going on out there, among the infinite worlds. "Wine," he called to a house-slave. "Bring me wine!"

~ ~ ~

In a sense, it would be like speaking from afar. Her father had already sent a part of himself somewhere. And it had remained.

As well as a part of her. It might be with Radal. Then she would need seek no further. She doubted this. A room. Black. She could see nothing, hear—what? Shuffling feet maybe. But Radal was here. Fachalana did not need to actually see him to know where he stood.

She bumped into something. A human form. Not Radal. And as herself, not completely there, so the sensations of touch were muted. It whispered words she could not understand, a language she did not know. There were more lost souls here than Radal's.

Father.

Fachalana. Go. Go. The voice was faint, far away, echoing into nothingness. *You are not here.*

No, she was not here, not with her father. She could sense the bonds that held him to the place, the bonds to Asak himself, a black web entangling what was Radal. *I will return for you,* she promised. Where to seek now?

She must seek herself, seek to speak from afar with that part of her that abode here. But—she was right here, not somewhere else.

When she looked, she saw only that part of her she had brought away from Drolwym. *Fachalana!* she cried out.

Fachalana! An echo or an answer? Send yourself, she thought. Send yourself to—to Fachalana. No, *into* Fachalana, sharing one space. She must do that to regain what she had lost.

Somewhere near but she could not connect. If only she could see! Fachalana reached out to another world, one of light, and pulled some of that light to her. There. Another Fachalana, a mirror reflecting her every movement, seeking to join even as did she. Now. Together. One space, one mind.

She was whole.

Who brings light here? Who dares?

She knew it was the voice of Asak. The god of death, of evil. Of emptiness and despair. She fled before its malice, its power, fled back to the place of power where she began her quest, barely knowing where she was.

Then Fachalana went to a place as black as the one she had just quit.

~ ~ ~

"It is Fachalana, isn't it?" asked Casurru.

Se answered honestly. "It is. She has gone to the cavern to seek what she has lost." She was glad Nel was off with her family, a league away. The girl would want to rush down there. "We will go down to her soon, but I do not wish to interfere with her concentration."

And, too, perhaps she feared the power beneath her feet. "She will need our aid when she is done."

"Should I tell Sir Blen?"

A sensible boy, he was. Rather like his Uncle Vantare. "Yes, do. Ansa and Donzalo, as well."

156

He hurried away. No need but no harm. Se said a prayer to Rema and, yes, to Esefa as well, for Fachalana's safety. But she knew that was all up to the woman herself.

~ ~ ~

Fachalana was groggy. Her wards were down as she returned to consciousness. One spoke to her; she knew she could put up her walls still. She had the strength.

I mean you no harm, came the voice. *I may not even be powerful enough if I wished.*

She could see him. He looked like a Laman peasant, somewhat, olive-skinned, dark close-cropped hair and beard. Even handsome, in a way. *Who are you?*

Call me simply the Asakian, for I am his priest. You are in the place of power where Nosana once stood. There was a long pause. *You are the daughter of Radal.* It was hard to tell if there was surprise.

He continued. *Nosana was manipulated by Radal but not really his minion.*

I knew this. She served the Lady of the Dark Moon and Asak.

She thought she heard the voice of Asak and in a way it was true. But it was the God of Darkness speaking through me. Dekata did speak to her, it is true. She likes the crazy ones.

Then you are the one who commanded her. I can hold you responsible for my sister's death.

He shrugged rather elegantly. *If you wish. I cared not one way or another about Jola. Her death served no purpose save that I always desire death. That is my duty as a follower of the Dark God. I thought to use the pitiable Nosana as a tool in other plots. That failed.*

Did you also seek to use Vis?

Ah, Vis. You are the one who broke up her little coven? Oh, of course

157

you are. I might have whispered in her ear a time or two. That wasn't so difficult in that place where you are.

Then we are enemies, I think.

We needn't be. I would rather you join us and wield your power in our cause.

I have seen Asak and he is no god I would follow.

Then I must warn you the next time we come together I may try to kill you. He seemed to be fading, breaking the connection. Then, of a sudden, he attacked, attempted to take what was her away from Fachalana and scatter it through the worlds.

He failed. There might have been the briefest moment of disorientation and then her protections were in place and the Asakian was expelled. Not blocked completely; she could still speak with him and felt secure in doing so. This was a new skill.

By Asak, you are strong, he hissed. *And I guess you know now that an Asakian will break any promise. In fact, it's expected of us!* He cackled a laugh and disappeared.

11

"I FOUND WHAT I sought. We can leave this place if you wish."

They had found her sleeping, quite peacefully, on her rug in the cavern. "You might need a little rest first," Blen told her.

"I always seemed to be worn out, don't I?" Fachalana laughed but then said, "I had not realized how much of myself I had lost. I am complete now. I am strong!"

He had always thought she was strong. "And you need risk yourself no more."

A hesitation, a dropping of her eyes, but then a look of resolve. "My father is still trapped in the realm of Asak. I must attempt to rescue him and give him peace." She couldn't have helped note his look of concern. "Oh, I'm not going to plunge back in anytime soon. There is so much I need to learn first."

"Learn where?" asked Ansa, at the door, Donzalo behind her.

"Some of the knowledge is in me. More is at my father's house, in the books there."

Donzalo spoke. "We're still a couple weeks from the Feast of Awakening. Maybe we could stay for it and then head south."

"Weather permitting," added Ansa.

"I'm told it's likely to change from hour to hour at this time of year," said Blen. He turned back to Fachalana. "But you must keep working on getting stronger."

"Right now," she told them all, "I am stronger than I have been since before my battle. Maybe stronger than I have every been."

That's pretty damned strong, Blen said only to himself.

~ ~ ~

"For the most part," admitted Pol, "I don't like men very much. Almost all of my friends are women."

"Men may feel the same about you. Especially when their women become your friends." Gos could be blunt when he wished. "Such as Princess Mara."

Odd the chief of the secret police would drop that name. Pol swished his wine about and thought a little while. "She very much loves her husband."

"And it seems Gawis loves her. Just walk cautiously, man."

The princess should be giving birth within the next couple weeks. He'd have to find a suitable gift to send. "I shall. At least Modareth doesn't mind my friendship with his wife." Not that he was at all close to the Princess Carrana. "I suppose he's one of those few men I like."

Did Gos wonder if he was one? He surely knew the answer was 'no' without asking. "I know you called me to discuss more than my friendships, male or female."

"The wizards are upset. Not just ours, They tell us their sort felt a disruption all over the world. Like what they used to feel when Lord Radal was up to something."

"And that matters to us?" He knew it did but wanted fat little Gos to tell him.

"The Lady Fachalana seems involved."

Now that was something. "She has not come to harm?"

"Not that anyone said. It's rumor, admittedly. Some of these sorcerers gossip with each other from a distance and stories get around to us." What was going on behind Gos's bland and blank expression? "The viscountess is your friend, I know. Another woman who likes you."

"And whom I like. And I'll tell you, Gos, her friends Sir Blen and Jobareth Nafal are among the few men I truly like."

The man might not believe him. It was Gos's job to be skeptical and he was very good at his job. "It is likely Fachalana will return to Sharsh soon. I can hope you will keep an eye on her."

So that was what all this was leading to. "It would be my pleasure," said Pol, and emptied his cup.

~ ~ ~

"Your brother is back."

Ansa followed Donzalo down the stairs—taking care not to stumble over one of the many cats of Drolwym—and into the broad hallway before the great main kitchen. My, it smelled good there!

There he was. Oder had his rebec with him, playing again the role of minstrel. Or was that his rebec? It looked different than she remembered.

The two of them, the siblings, looked somewhat alike. Donzalo had noted that at once and made the connection between them— even though she had dyed her blond hair dark when first they met. It was blond again now and had been for some time. Still a bit short for her having cropped it last year, when she traveled disguised as a boy. Oder's remained long and very blond, almost white.

Both he greeted with an embrace. "I will come to see you at Felewym soon. Perhaps it will be last my last time traveling through these lands as a bard. There will be much to discuss then. But for now," he continued, giving the instrument an idle strum, "I am here only to spend the Feast of Awakening with my friends."

A clump of children had gathered, among them Nel, with her mother. Ansa thought it likely some of the youngsters were Fausala's other children, the 'terrors.' "Oder, Oder," one called, "sing us a song." They knew the minstrel Oder, who had at times visited here in the past with Guesare. Of the spy Oder they knew nothing and it is unlikely they cared.

"Very well. Gather round here." They sat on the floor, a ring of eager faces looking to him.

> *Giants don't watch where they step;*
> *their focus is not on the ground.*
> *You might yell, 'Hey, we're down here!'*
> *but those giants won't hear a sound.*
> *They flatten what lies in their path,*
> *and thump on wherever they're bound;*
> *so make sure your house isn't built*
> *where giants might be around.*

There the Ani minstrel plucked a sequence of thumping notes on the low strings, emulating the steps of those giants. Ansa had always known him to play the rebec with his bow, not his fingers. That had been Guesare's way.

> *Giants don't watch where they step*
> *no need when one's that big and strong.*
> *They amble with heads in the clouds;*
> *they bumble and fumble along.*
> *You may not know one is coming,*
> *till you hear them roaring a song,*
> *so if they do step on your house,*
> *they didn't mean to do wrong.*

It is to be noted that more than one little boy was stomping about, giant-fashion, by the end.

"Did you make that up?" asked Nel.

"No, child. It was one of your father's songs. And this," he said, holding up the instrument, "was your father's rebec. It should be yours now." His eyes went to Fausala, who nodded.

Not that she would forbid it now. Her brother knew what he was doing when it came to manipulating people.

"Let's go in and get some breakfast," she said.

~ ~ ~

She would never ride Jola's horse again. This she knew. Fachalana galloped across the rounded hills, not caring where the gray stallion carried her.

Tomorrow was the Feast of Awakening, the day halfway between the Yule and the Spring Equinox. A day celebrated as the return of spring, though cold and miserable weather might linger for some time.

And when the feasting was done there would come goodbyes and they would leave the Cuddon.

The morning was still. Mist lingered in the hollows of the hills. The cottage, the graves, lay before her. This is where the horse had chosen to bear her. Fachalana dismounted and stood a minute by the two graves, that of Guesare, that of Jola. Jola, sister to both her and Guesare. That made him a brother, didn't it? She would think of him so from now on.

The stallion nuzzled her, whinnied softly, turned to canter away. She watched until it could be seen no longer.

Fachalana began the walk back to Drolwym. This, also, she would never do again.

Of Homecomings: The Third Tale

1

LOMELA HAD KNOWN they were coming, of course. As soon as the party followed the Great Road across the borders of County Rosam, a swift messenger had come to her with the news. After a short debate with herself, she let Jobareth know about it too.

Doufan would learn when he learned.

She saw the signal flag wave at the first of Rosam Castle's three gates. "They're here," she informed her lover. "Let's go down to the courtyard to greet them."

Jobareth Nafal grimaced. "Couldn't we greet them indoors where it's warm?"

But she was already out the door. He would follow her.

On the steps before the the Great Hall they waited, Lomela wrapped in a russet shawl. She knew it went well with her hair color. Jobareth stood just slightly behind her. When they were married they would stand side by side, but until then decorum prevented it. Not that everyone in the keep didn't know he shared her bed.

Her bed, not her bedroom. That too must wait. Here they came through the final gateway, beneath the iron portcullis. Four riders, four friends. Her best friends—they and this fellow next to her. Behind her.

She loved no others as much, save maybe her brother Modareth, far off in Sharsh. And, to be sure, her father the king and her little Ros. She should have brought him down here with her. Dame Traspa had him somewhere around the place.

Oh, this was stupid, to stand up here. Down the steps she went, Jobareth in her wake, to throw her arms around Fachalana, and then each of the others in turn. Yes, Blen too, even if it made him uncomfortable!

"Now come inside, all of you, before Jobareth starts complaining of the cold again."

"That's like him," commented Fachalana. "I'll have you know, Jobo, we rode many leagues through worse weather."

"And we have many more leagues ahead of us," said Blen.

"Not right away, I hope! How long can you remain with me? A day, a week? All summer?" That last was unlikely but she might as well ask.

Donzalo answered. "Ansa and I will not bide long here, I am sorry to say. We should be off to our new home in a couple days."

"But it's close enough we can visit. My husband has promised me we will," said Ansa.

"I believe I said only that it was possible. We will certainly be able to visit my uncle from time to time. We'll stop there on our way."

"And you two?" asked Lomela, turning to Blen and Fachalana. They walked together like a couple. Would the knight accompany her to Sharsh?

"We're in no hurry," Fachalana assured her. "A week or two? I don't know."

Before Spring Feast. She had hoped they could stay that long but had known it was unlikely.

"That could also depend on when Lord Doufan is ready to leave," said Jobareth. "The king told him to make sure you made it safely to Sharsh."

"It's more likely to be the other way around!"

"I hope he doesn't insist on a litter," was all Blen had to say about it.

~ ~ ~

She wasn't likely to be invited to this royal naming either. Mara's child was even more important than Princess Carrana's. A boy—the heir Prince Gawis had so long awaited!

Celatas was abuzz with the news. Rumor was the little lad would be named Greneth, after his great-grandfather, the Liberator, the man who drove the Ani from Sharsh. That wouldn't be known for sure until the ceremony.

The other rumor going about was that Viscountess Fachalana was finally returning. It was not rumor to Erlana; she had her brother's letter telling her of it. She did wish he would write in more detail! What good being a poet if one didn't use plenty of words?

Like the playwright Pol. She had to admit she liked his comedies better than her brother's play. Erlana had seen 'Oemse' staged and had not been impressed. Nor, it seemed, had been the critics of Celatas. It was good of Pol to mount the play for him, though. He was a friend of Jobareth—in fact, his protege at one time. A friend of Lady Fachalana too.

Maybe she could get her to introduce them when she arrived. She wouldn't mind having the acquaintance of the handsome Pol at all. Quite unattached, Erlana was assured. Oh, maybe he didn't like girls! That would be dreadful!

She should write a play herself. Why not? She wouldn't be the first woman to have her work acted on the stages of the capital. But write about what? Erlana sucked at her pen, considered the many possibilities. Oh, none of those were any good. She restrained herself from throwing the pen across the room.

How about the story Jobareth had told them about Godos Tasetha? It could be embellished a bit. Not smugglers. Pirates! The adventure of a boy kidnapped by pirates. She dipped the stylus in her ink pot and began.

~ ~ ~

"I must hear all your stories," said Lomela.

Nafal laughed at this, but in good nature. "Wouldn't one of them be enough?

"A tale is but half told when only one person tells it," spoke Godos.

Doufan raised an eyebrow. "That is starting to become annoying, boy."

Someone should have said the same to the ambassador long ago, thought Fachalana.

"We'll give you what we can before we leave," promised Donzlo. "The day after tomorrow. Early." He looked to Ansa who nodded a vigorous agreement.

"But we're in not such a hurry," Fachalana assured her.

"I'll leave that up to you and Sir Blen, my dear," said Doufan. "I can be ready to leave at a day's notice."

"Hey, don't I get a say?"

"No, Godos, you do not," the ambassador told him.

They talked on a while, but all were somewhat weary. Doufan and young Tasetha—he did seem a somewhat changed boy— discreetly took their leave and Ansa and Donzlo found their room and, one assumed, their bed. Fachalana didn't feel like sleeping yet.

"I'm going to walk along the ramparts, I think," she said. "I've never looked out over the western walls at night." Those rose atop the cliffs, high above Ros-town.

Blen rose. "May I accompany you, my lady?"

"I would welcome it, sir."

Very formal, but there was a current of playfulness running

beneath their words, as if they were each teasing the other. Side by side they climbed to the highest battlements—all three walls grew closer together as one moved westward, until the outer ones narrowed to no more than catwalks above the cliffs.

"This is where Donzalo was almost thrown over," spoke Blen, coming to a halt and leaning against the crenelated wall. "It's a pretty good view too."

"Which was why he dawdled here that night. I've had the spot pointed out to me as well." She leaned forward beside him, gazing out toward the river, the lights of the town. "Almost two years ago."

"And rescued by Guesare. It has always been assumed the brothers Perdos and Percos were his attackers but naught was proven."

At the orders of her father. Neither would bring that up. "It will be good to rest here a week or so."

"Yes. Um, you don't intend to tire yourself again, do you?"

Such a roundabout way to ask if she would practice sorcery! "I think I shall not poke into any world but this one until I am in Sharsh. For now, I would rather enjoy my time with Lomela, and the road is no place for such things."

"What sort of things is it for?" asked Blen.

They stared at each other. We must look very foolish, thought Fachalana. Then Blen took her into his arms and she went eagerly, his mouth seeking her own.

About time. She rather suspected Blen was thinking the same.

~ ~ ~

Some trees were budding out. Some were even blooming, pink and white showing on either side of their road.

Grippo was a good companion. Ansa was glad the hierophant gave him permission to come along. It would give him a chance to visit his mother, and his brother's family. "Wild plums," he said, pointing to a snowy bush. "They'll grow anywhere."

"But fruit fit only for birds," replied Donzalo.

"The birds need to eat as much as you and I."

"But you don't eat birds, do you, Brother?" asked a soldier riding near them.

"I could. I've yet to take my vows." He grinned. "And when my sister-in-law's cooking is set before me, I'm likely to forget them entirely!"

They rode with one of the regular patrols and would take the four days Rosam troops usually did to traverse this road. Yes, they could have ridden faster, camped more lightly, but no one felt a need to hurry. And the soldiers would feed them.

Beyond Sir Paren's keep, they would be on their own.

Around noon on the fourth day, fields opened up on either side of the way, some pasturage, some land lying fallow until spring planting. Barns, then cottages. Ahead, through the trees, the walls of Paren's modest keep could be spied, and the good-sized village sprung up around it. Too close to it, some said. It made the place less defensible.

A little girl by the road, a white dog at her side. "King!" called Ansa, and slid from her mount. The dog frisked to her. "And Ramapa." The girl might not remember her as well as her dog did.

"Your Uncle Grippo is here," she told her.

Grippo joined them and hoisted the girl into his arms. "Come and say hello to King," she called to her husband.

"I've been a bit leery of white dogs since Radal sent a pack of them after me," Donzalo called from his horse. He was attempting to sound serious about it. Ansa was not in the least fooled.

"That's a sorry jest, sir," she told him. "And this fellow has a heart of pure gold. No devil-dog in you, is there, King?" She ruffled his fur again and rose. "We must have many dogs at our new home."

"Black ones," stipulated Donzalo, who had dismounted to walk beside them. "Or maybe brown."

2

"THEY HAVEN'T DONE anything, my lady, as far as I can tell. Stick to their own rooms and just smooch here and there when they think no one's looking."

If anyone knew what was going on in Castle Rosam, from the stables to the kitchens to the upper hallways, it was Dame Traspa.

"I fear they are complete novices, Traspa," replied Countess Lomela. "We must give them time to figure things out."

"I never needed any time," muttered Traspa. "Careful with that, little sir!"

"What have we there?"

"Sword!" crowed Ros. "Blayum gave me." He waved it back and forth in a menacing manner. She was certain Ros considered it menacing, at any rate.

It was of wood and rather well made. Blunt, of course. "Sir Blen carved it for the lad," said Traspa. "The man is surprisingly talented with his hands." She snickered. "Let us hope Lady Fachalana gets to find out about that."

"Traspa!" She shook her head, following the gesture with a sigh. "Both leave us tomorrow. All my friends will be far away."

"Not Jobareth, my lady. I think maybe he is the one you most care about."

That was so. She and Jobareth, together, serving this people who had become her people, rearing her son. Maybe more children, in time. "I think Blen became his best friend at some point. Were I not absolutely certain the man would refuse, I would offer him a position here."

Traspa nodded knowingly. "Sir Blen will serve only the Lady Fachalana."

Though she loved Fachalana, she was not convinced of Blen's

wisdom in this. Ah, the two had their own destiny to fashion. "Sir! You are slaying my favorite cushion!"

"Dragum," Ros corrected. "Dead dragum."

~ ~ ~

A square, squat tower of gray stone occupied one corner, making up a part of the wall.

"Your Felewym is a tower-house castle," said Oder. "The tower there was built by we Ani, to keep a watch on you dangerous Lamans. In time, we abandoned fortifications of this sort and one local leader or another occupied it. Bandits, sorcerers. The outer wall was added at some point."

"And they incorporated the tower into it." Donzalo wasn't certain he approved. It seemed inelegant.

"Simpler. Less stone, less work."

The Ani had been awaiting their arrival; that surprised neither Ansa nor Donzalo. More surprising was that he had a crew of Cuddonians there making repairs on the tumbling-down keep.

"The place was not in such bad shape," Oder assured them. "The walls are mostly solid, except there at the top of tower." He pointed to gaps in the stonework. "Filthy, though, and a lot of the timber was bad."

"I don't suppose Sabatare gave much attention to maintenance."

"The folk here said the wizard shut himself away and was rarely seen. Then Radal's men camped here and thoroughly trashed the place." Oder and Donzalo had come on the keep not long after the mercenary band had vacated it. "The neighbors did not like their presence at all. At least the wizard didn't bother them."

"But now they will have a doughty knight to protect them," spoke Ansa.

Oder smiled at his sister's half-jest. "So they hope. Most people prefer a bit of security in their lives. But you'll have to do more than that to get by here. The farm lands have long lain fallow but are ready again for the plow."

Farming? In time. He needed to learn exactly how much land he could lay claim to. Felewym lay in a valley among the high hills of the southern Cuddon. This was the southern Cuddon, wasn't it? Maybe more the central Cuddon. These hills extended nearly to the Lesser Sea but somewhere they ceased to wear the name of Cuddon. The coast down there, east of Morparas, was indisputably Anian.

Sheep grazed on the steep grassy slopes. He must learn his relationship to the shepherds as well. They were likely to think of the valley as their own. "I'll have to put in a gate sometime. Walls without a gate aren't very useful."

"And stables and storehouses and much more. I don't suppose it's ready to move into?" Ansa asked her brother.

"We'll need to finish rebuilding the floors. So come along, Donzalo. We can use another strong back for the work."

"Yes, go be useful for something. I think I will ride out and see what's to be seen."

"And let yourself be seen, in turn," said Oder. "The folk here will be curious."

"I'll try to make a good impression," she promised.

~ ~ ~

Blen was relieved to find Lord Doufan did not insist on a horse litter. So had the nobleman traveled from Sharsh to Lama, by Nafal's report. His friend believed he had done so only to impress on his companions that he would have his own way in things.

There was a wagon, however. A cart, perhaps, better described it. Doufan's scribe rode in it, as one or the other of the two soldiers assigned to them—Sharshite soldiers from the embassy—took a turn at the reins.

"I could readily have left everything behind," declared the former ambassador. "Save my secretary! I care little for the odds and ends we carry back to Sharsh."

And so they rode, northwestward toward the King's Pass, the door to Sharsh. "You would know this road well, Blen," said Doufan.

"That I do, sir. I traveled it frequently as a courier." And a few times since. Would he ever again? His life would be remade in Sharsh.

Across the Weldar they traveled, taking the ferry at Ros-town, and the lands of County Rosam in time gave way to those of Count Dordos. Other counties lay further on, and Blen neither remembered nor cared who ruled in them. Doufan's diplomatic credentials took them across borders without fuss. The rolling countryside was turning green around them, farm and forest coming to life on either side of their road. It was a good road, though dirt most of its length, and well-maintained in every land through which they passed.

It is not a journey of a few days from County Rosam to Sharsh, but of weeks. At least when one must stick to the pace of a one-horse cart. But in time their road joined with the wide King's Road, the stone-paved highway leading east to Oles and west to the pass.

They rode and at Blen's side rode Fachalana.

~ ~ ~

Fronos Tasetha was a rarity in Sharsh, at least among men of his class. He was a Kamatian, a convert in his youth, who had traveled to Oles and had been impressed by the faith and ways of that city's people. Hard-working, sober folk they were.

As for the gods of his own people, he cared not one way or

another. They seemed a frivolous bunch. They certainly had no claim to the worship of any man.

He looked again at the letter he held. Not from his son but from Lord Doufan. The diplomat seemed to have taken the boy under his wing. Kamat knew why! Fronos was not sure whether he approved; still, friends in high places could be a good thing. Not that he'd needed any. He had built his fleet and his fortune quite on his own.

"By this," he told his wife, "the boy might already be at King's Pass."

"And what shall we do with him when he gets home at last?" she asked. "It seems he is no longer the boy we sent off to sea."

Indeed. There was no telling how Godos might view any plans they had for his future. "He is still my son. He will do what I tell him."

His wife shot a most doubtful look at him.

Fronos had to laugh. "I know, I know. He was not obedient before. There is no telling how independent and how stubborn he will return to us."

"As stubborn as his father, maybe?"

"Maybe! I say we introduce him to as many suitable young women as we can to distract the boy. Marriage will settle him down."

He couldn't tell whether his wife believed that.

3

"I DIDN'T EXPECT the king to be here."

Around a spur of the mountains, the Zadcelam, the ramparts of Mountain Keep had become suddenly visible, rising above the entry to the pass into Sharsh. Strictly, this little strip of Lama through which they rode was a part of the kingdom of Sharsh.

Fachalana turned baffled eyes to him. "How do you know?"

"His banner." He pointed it out. "It flies above the fortress."

There *was* a flag and it *was* the king's green and argent. She would take Blen's word that it meant Lareth was in residence.

"I suspect it is you he has come to meet, my lady, rather than me," remarked Doufan.

"And definitely not me," Godos added.

"You he might turn back at the border," Fachalana told him.

They climbed toward the massive keep. That tower there had been her father's. Rumors of his magics in its upper rooms were whispered through the halls of Mountain Keep and some might have had truth to them. Not so long ago, she would not have given them much credence, before she knew the ways of sorcery herself.

The reeve of the keep, Lareth's deputy here, greeted them. "The king may call for you later," he told them, "but he knows you will be weary from your journey. Come; there are rooms prepared."

Fachalana hoped they were on the side of the castle that received some sunlight. Even better if there were windows! Mountain Keep could be a cold place, much of it cut from the mountain itself, the rest stones piled atop.

"Sir Reeve," she said, "could I visit Lord Radal's old rooms? Or is that prohibited?"

"Ah, my lady, the truth is one knows how to get in. We have no key and the lock has baffled all attempts at its picking."

"There might be wards on it." She need think no more than a second on that. "No, there are certainly wards on it. I can take a look. And—" Oh, you're being dramatic, she told herself as soon as she paused. You're not on the stage at Celatas! "I might just know where my father hid a key."

"I shall ask the king if he will permit it," he promised.

Servants showed them to their quarters, all close, opening onto the same hallway. Even that of Godos. Fachalana hoped the king did not call. She needed some sleep and her legs and rear end hurt from being overlong in the saddle.

Blen came to the open door, hesitating there a moment before deciding not to enter. "I'll be right across the way if you need me," he said. She but nodded. She might need him sometime but not right now!

The key. She knew exactly where it was hidden. Did she know this from her father's memories or was it written down in his papers at their villa? Papers she shouldn't have been able to find and peruse —Radal had been astounded she had. More so in that he hadn't known she had powers at all!

Nor had she. She had swept aside his wards without realizing they were there.

Well, that was for later. Lady Fachalana slipped into her comfortable feather bed and then into sleep.

~ ~ ~

Galaro and his traders had departed County Rosam well before the travelers to Sharsh. Now they made their way slowly south on the Great Road, stopping here and there to offer their wares.

"Are we going all the way down t' the coast for more merchandise?" asked his second.

He hadn't quite decided. Galaro suspected the best days of the smuggling business might be in the past. The coasts were not as open and lawless as once they had been. It was some time since he had personally slipped across the strait to Lorj.

If this union of the Partanacans and Coradeans came off, it might be even harder to bring goods in. Why, they might do better just to go to Pas or Arlacas and buy the stuff legitimately. He could see himself settling in permanently in a place like that, opening a shop, leaving the roads.

Or a tavern, as had Perdos. *Galaro's Grub and Grog* had a good ring to it.

No, not yet. Galaro was far from weary of traveling. "Spring Feast is not too far away," he said, as much to himself as his companion. "We should pick a good market to visit on the holiday."

The man laughed and squinted his good eye at him. "The place we left a coupla weeks ago is better 'n most."

"And we'll get back there for the Summer Fair. With all the troubles over in County Rosam, it should be profitable again."

"As long as the new countess doesn't raise the fees even higher 'n Borrago," opined his lieutenant.

~ ~ ~

Right there. Fachalana removed a small panel in the thick oak door frame and retrieved the key. Rather small, wasn't it? She'd half-expected something more impressive, like that which unlocked the Chamber of Dreams.

"That's been there all along?" asked the reeve. "How did we miss it?"

"There was a bond set on it." It had looked like just a part of the frame. The spell had been quite simple; her father had not meant it to keep anyone out, just to make sure the key wasn't misplaced.

The lock would be another matter. In she slipped the key. Ah, the tumblers were all gummed up with bindings. It would take a few seconds to pick them apart. There. The key turned, the heavy ebony and brass door swung inward.

The first floor was Radal's office. This was far from being at the ground floor of the keep, but already well up. One could see far from its slit of a window, east into Lama.

"Someone might want to look at the papers here," spoke the reeve.

Fachalana nodded and looked toward the staircase. "He never let anyone go further than this room."

"I know his henchman Sojel was permitted down here," said Blen. None other accompanied them, save a pair of guards in the hall.

"Ansa and I were in here too. Let's see what's on the second floor."

The reeve spoke. "I will not intrude, my lady." His eyes went to her companion.

"Sir Blen comes with me."

The next floor held spare living quarters, a narrow bed, some chests, a small desk. "He slept here, I think. When he slept."

The room at the top of the tower, behind another heavy door, was open to the air of the mountains, a colonnade running all around the space. "I would come up here just for the view," she whispered. Maybe she would sometime. But now—

Papers and instruments, bowls, casks, were scattered on a long table of dark marble. Blen leafed through a few of the papers. "There doesn't seem to be a great deal of importance to any of them. Some old documents, some jottings on this and that."

"No grimoire," she said. It was slightly disappointing but not unexpected. Radal's small book of knowledge, the one he carried when traveling, had been destroyed, burnt, in the battle at Rosam

Castle. The large one was probably in his office at home. Was that sealed too?

Fachalana returned to the view. "This is where my father stood, waiting to be borne away by a dragon. Knowing he could never return, that he had broken the last bonds to Sharsh. To Lareth."

"He might have called that red demon to him here, too."

"The one Donzalo slew on the road to Drolwym. The Rupa." They had both heard the story, from more than one mouth. "There is nothing here," Fachalana said, turning away. "Let's go see what's happening in this place. And," she continued, "if there's naught to do, you must fence with me. I need some exercise!"

"Then, my lady, you should find someone more skilled to face."

4

It was a mean hut of stone and earth, deep in the hills. Vis had fled far from Drolwym, far from the lands of Thane Vantare and those of his neighbors. Word of her would have been passed to them. They would have been watching.

Not here. This rounded *shieling*, a shepherds' humble dwelling, was safe. None sought her here. It would do for the coming summer. She could make a meager living off the land until the cold came again. After that? Vis didn't know.

But already she was getting a reputation as a wise woman, as a teller of fortunes and seer of the future. She knew potions that could cure a stomach ache or remove an undesirable mate. A witch, a mean little witch of the wild Cuddon. Was that to be her future?

This place was not so far from the old abode of the sorcerer Sabatare. It would be amusing to some, perhaps, that friends of the hated Fachalana, the Fachalana who so outshone her, lived there now. Felewym they had named the place, the House of the Wolf.

That was undoubtedly a reference to the goddess Diba. She seemed to be a patron of this Donzalo, as she had been to Jola. Who was that, skulking? Ah, a little goblin. They peeped at her from time to time. Didn't Sabatare have friends among the Other Folk?

She should try to befriend them herself. Any allies would be welcome now.

~ ~ ~

"I would ask you two to look over Radal's belongings. The papers, in particular." Lareth looked from Doufan to Blen. "I can't think of any better suited to the task."

"And we happen to be on hand, sire?" ask Doufan.

The king chuckled. "Yes, that too, sir. Now get yourselves out of here. I wish to speak with the viscountess."

The two, young noblewoman, elderly monarch, settled into cushioned chairs before the hearth. "Have you plans for your return to Sharsh, my lady?" he asked.

"I feel like I am starting all over. And my best friends are elsewhere."

"Yet you do have many friends here. My son is your friend. And that protege of his who is making such a stir."

She must have appeared perplexed. She felt perplexed.

"Pol. The one who took over your theater and is the darling of half the noblewomen in Celatas."

"Oh! He was Jobareth's protege before he was Prince Modareth's."

"I think he need be no one's protege now. Jobareth—I assume he will marry my daughter."

She couldn't help smiling. Maybe even smirking. "I am sure Lord Doufan has already told you all about that, sir."

"Indeed. Jobareth is a good lad. Maybe Lomela should have married him in the first place! It would have saved everyone a great deal of trouble these past two years." Both knew the political realities would not have permitted it. "I am grateful for the friendship he showed my son. Modareth was painfully shy when small, and a stutterer. It was for his sake I allowed Jobareth Nafal the run of the place, to be a companion to him. A lad of his own age and almost as bookish, but more outgoing and self-assured."

"It worked. But I was there too, you know."

"I fear you frightened Modareth more than you helped him. You could be quite the bully, Fachalana."

She wasn't about to deny it. "And Jobo didn't hesitate to put me in my place."

"He helped you too. I believe you were as unsure of yourself as my son."

Maybe the king was right about that. Maybe a part of her still felt unsure.

"So," he continued, "marriages. Are you to wed Sir Blen?"

She did not hesitate. "Yes, once he proposes. Or I propose. I am sure one or the other will happen."

"No doubt. I might have expected a higher-born match for you." She could not read the king. Did he mean to object?

"My grandfather was but a mercenary and refugee," she protested. It was true, though, that her family had married into the Sharshite nobility.

"Expected, I said. Not hoped for. I can think of few men better than Blen. It is well you waited for him, though your—" Lareth stopped short. Thinking better of his words?

"My father you were going to to say. Yes, he despaired of me ever marrying."

"Perhaps this will help give him peace."

No. There was another path Fachalana must follow to bring her father peace. She would say nothing of that to the king.

But she must step soon onto that path.

~ ~ ~

Rumors swirled about Celatas about the health of the infant heir. Some said he was seriously ill. Some said he had died.

Erlana's sister-in-law had not been invited to the naming cere-mony but they did know now he had been given the name Greneth. That was known everywhere. Greneth the Second he would be someday, the gods permitting.

"You've been writing all day, dear," said her mother.

"I want to get it finished before Lady Fachalana arrives," she replied. "Well, not finished. Presentable." Word had come the viscountess was at the border of Sharsh, at Mountain Keep. And the king had even gone to meet her!

"She may be too busy to look at your play."

That was what she feared. But she was a friend of Jobareth, right? Maybe she could make some time for his sister.

Or maybe Erlana should recognize she wasn't really a writer and go spend time with her friends. There were plenty enough balls to fill ones time and the theaters would remain open for a while yet. And then summer would bring other entertainments. And young men.

"I'm going to do my best on it, anyway," she declared. She might never get another chance.

~ ~ ~

One or the other would propose. That was what she told the king. It didn't matter; both she and Blen knew they were going to wed.

Words spoken or unspoken would not change that. She faced the man, sword drawn, over the green lawn of the practice yard. "On guard, sir!"

Blen did his best to present a defense. He was quite hopeless, wasn't he? But he was a capable fighting man as a soldier, resolute, courageous. He could hack away with the best of them! That would have to be enough.

"No, you should have watched my tip." She wasn't sure what he had been looking at.

"My mind is not in fencing today, my lady."

She glared at him. "Sorry. I know you are not 'my lady' when we are at swords."

"I need never be 'my lady' to you, Blen."

He made a practice pass with his blade. "Then perhaps you will be my wife."

"Gladly. I already have the king's consent."

"That was necessary? And he gave permission before I asked?"

"Oh, everyone knew you would. It might or might not be required, what with me being a noblewoman and dependent on no one and that sort of thing."

"And well of age to be your own mistress."

"True. Old enough that I need no kinsman's approval, but a king is different. Especially one that made me a viscountess!"

"Oh, then you were just worried about losing the income that comes with the title."

"That will be your income too, my lad. Now—have at you!"

5

It had been too brief, his time with his family. A part of Grippo wished to turn around, return to the manor of Sir Paren, forget the priesthood.

Yet he believed he had a calling. Religion was integral to him; perhaps not serving in some village shrine but study and learning, the pursuit of moral and theological questions. Where could he do that save in the priesthood?

Among those who followed the southern pontifex, the one in Lorj, the priesthood was not celibate. That sounded rather good to Grippo. Doing without women had always been a sticking point— not that some priests didn't have mistresses.

That wouldn't do for him. It would not be enough and he would take his vows seriously.

The hierophant was no longer dictating. Or maybe he had been and Grippo hadn't been listening. "Brother Grippo," he said, "what shall we do with you after midsummer?"

"That is yours to command, your grace."

"Yes, of course, but it is no answer. I could make you an instructor at the seminary. You're well suited."

But young. No man freshly ordained would be given such a post.

"Perhaps Donzalo—they style him Laird now, right? Perhaps Donzalo would like to have a priest in residence at his manor. You could be a missionary to the Cuddonians."

Was the man serious? Grippo had not heard good things of what Cuddonians did to Kamatian missionaries. Not anything fatal, thank Kamat, but uncomfortable. "A priest at his uncle's keep could visit him from time to time."

"Indeed. The one there now is far too lazy, I am afraid. Not that he is a bad man. But, my boy, I wouldn't send you there. You'd end up lazy too."

"Most likely, your grace. My mother would spoil me."

"Or you could remain my secretary. You are rather useful."

"Thank you, your grace." Not that he didn't know it.

"Now where were we? Oh, yes, a letter to our brother at Oles." The hierophant shook his head. "Such an idiot. And to think I voted for him!"

~ ~ ~

Fachalana climbed to the top of her father's tower. The cold here she had expected, and had appropriated a long and heavy fur robe from a wardrobe in a storeroom. Whose it was, she had no idea.

Clear skies, overflowing with stars, greeted her. She hooded her lantern so its light was barely to be noticed and sat, looking out into the night. She had come with no other plan.

She need do nothing; this Fachalana knew. Her father had chosen his fate. She could forget him, live her life with the man she loved. She could forget and forego magic altogether.

Fachalana breathed in the crisp, clean air of the mountains. This was what life was truly about! Such sensations, the bright stars of these heights, the rolling power of the sea, the scent of the pine forest. The taste of wine and—the taste of a man's lips on her own. She needed that. She needed it all, she realized.

But first, she let herself seek into the night, seek the Plain of Silver, shining as brightly as the stars. She would stay there, just a little while, and find its peace before returning to the turbulent, busy, intoxicating world. All around her it spread.

There were no words, yet it was almost as if she carried on a conversation with it, as if the Plain itself were sentient. She knew nothing of its nature. Who might she ask?

Reluctantly, gradually, she let herself drift away and back to herself in the tower. Who was that? Some sorcerer or another had briefly touched her mind. That was not so unusual.

Fachalana had confidence in her strength now. She would no longer hide from every voice, secure in her wardings. *I greet you.*

Hi, came a cheerful voice

Hi, came a second one.

Two women materialized in the world she had chosen for their meeting. Blond hair, but the faces were as dark as her own. Slim. Age? She couldn't decide.

Speak Ani do you? asked one

I am afraid not.

Muram all right, said the other. *Ispa I am.*

And Ilma.

Twins, she decided. Possibly Ani, but they didn't look like any she had ever met. She should assume nothing.

Radal daughter, said Ilma. Or Ispa.

We Radal know.

Knew, her sister corrected. *Muram past tense.*

Oh. Send him rupa!

You know the rupa? asked Fachalana.

They what word? Pet? Maybe.

Bother not us. Just men.

Take to nests and sex have!

And what do the men think of that?

Don't know.

Don't care.

Fun watch!

Fachalana felt that a good moment to return to herself.

~ ~ ~

She is not much of a tool but I shall not throw her aside, the Asakian decided. Vis might prove useful yet.

She had not the true devotion to Asak, the devotion to doing evil wherever and whenever, to spreading pain and death and despair. To desire the end of being.

Vis, he called.

She had some trouble getting enough of herself there, remaining transparent, wavering, for a while. Vis was not a strong sorceress and she could no longer depend on her cavern, her place of power. *I haven't heard from you in a while*, she said.

You look thinner.

Short rations, Asakian. I live in a hovel in the wilderness.

I had heard you left Drolwym. Nothing more.

And should you know more?

A challenge? *If we are to serve Asak we must work together.*

I think I choose to serve myself now. Little good Asak did for me.

Asak does not do good, he reminded her. *We serve him and expect naught but death.*

He could blast the woman right now, while she was open to him. She had not the strength to resist. It tempted so, to feel her anguish, her despair, as she was torn away from herself and scattered across the void—

No, no, she might, indeed, prove useful yet. *Perhaps we shall speak again*, said the Asakian, as he faded.

~ ~ ~

Oil lamps cast pools of soft golden light along the way. Enough to find her way back to her room. This fur felt uncomfortably hot now. She dropped it to the floor as soon as she was inside.

Fachalana turned, her eyes going to the door across the hall. If she hesitated at all, it was for but a second before crossing. "Blen?" she whispered, pushing it a little ajar.

"Yes, I'm here."

"Did I wake you?" She felt her resolve slipping.

"No, Fachalana. I've been lying here thinking." A moment of silence. "Thinking of you."

"And I was thinking of you." She slipped into the chamber. "Or of you and me."

"You and me. Is it true? Will it be you and me?"

"Forever and ever," she solemnly intoned and then giggled. "Or until you're old and fat and some young fellow comes along."

"I'll challenge him to a duel. I might know how to fence by then."

The edge of his bed. She took a seat. So close he was, there in the darkness. "You know I'm not going to leave you tonight either."

His answer was to reach out, pull her to him. "Tonight or any night," she whispered, as she slid beneath the covers. "Forever and ever."

6

GALARO'S SECOND STEPPED from the Todmouth ferry. He'd sent him ahead to check on opportunities before choosing to cross here.

"No other traders," the man reported. "or none what matter. Should do good business. News is Oba kicked her last bucket and her place is up for sale."

Galaro nor his men had ever frequented Mistress Oba's dive. He preferred *The Truculent Troll*, or even *The Count's Cow*, on the far side of town.

"All her whores turned out?"

"Not yet. No one in charge to do it. Oba's place had a good location, whatever else one may say of it. Or of her."

Galaro would speak no ill of the dead, though all spoke ill enough of Oba when alive! "Right on the river it is," he mused. "Yes, a good location and not just for a tavern and whore house."

"Yes, Captain. That's why I was thinking of buying it."

Every man left the road eventually. Why not this one? "You've enough saved?"

"That I do. Some of it with a banker over there." He nodded toward the far side of Weldar.

Galaro nodded as well. So be it. "Let's get everything across. We'll set up for two or three days and then move on. And if you don't come with us, lad, I wish you the best of luck."

"Thanks, sir. Will y' be going on up to Orgelo's place then?" The two strolled toward the waiting troop, men, horses, wagons.

"Too soon for Tod-ford again. Even my brother may be sick of seeing me. We'll go down the west side of the river a distance before cutting away. I've contacts down there I could be looking up."

Galaro was not ready to give up quite yet on smuggling.

~ ~ ~

It would be up to Blen to deal with the condition of his room. No one had seen her leaving it! Still, she felt that people were staring at her as she made her way to King Lareth's private chambers. It was time to discuss moving on to Celatas after these three days of rest.

She stopped suddenly, puzzled, when she entered the room. It felt like a place of power was near. Something like a place of power. She had not felt that here before.

That ebony chest on Lareth's desk. Hadn't that been her father's? She never knew what lay within it.

"What is the matter, my lady?"

She pointed at the cask. "Where did that come from?"

"It was among your father's effects that came back with Doufan. There was little more than it and a few papers, a deck of cards. It was all bundled and brought here."

"It has power. I am not sure how." She had never even heard of such a thing.

"And you did not feel it during your travels? It was with you all the way."

She had not. "I think it might be necessary to be very close to it. What is inside?" They had surely looked.

"A skull. Nothing more. Would you like me to have it removed?" Lareth sounded concerned; despite knowing of her father's magics, he had not seen her practice them.

"Yes, please, your highness. Maybe send it along to my father's— ah, to my villa and I'll try to figure out what it is when I get there."

"Or I could order it destroyed," spoke the king. "It might be the better choice." She had no answer for that. Maybe she agreed, yet it might hold some of the knowledge she sought. "I shall order your villa unsealed when you arrive in Celatas. When we arrive; we shall journey back together." He regarded the box. "This I shall send immediately. Ho," he called to one of the servants, "remove this to, ah, the reeve's chambers."

Fachalana had indeed felt nothing, sensed nothing, during the trip from Castle Rosam. She'd had her warding up, keeping out everything, with not one thought of magic.

With the box gone from the room, she could again forget such things. "So," spoke King Lareth, "will you be ready to leave on the morrow?"

"I shall, sir. May I ask—may I ask what plans you might have for Sir Blen?" He was a soldier of the king, after all.

"I am not going to send him to another distant posting! Have no fear of that, my lady. In truth, I would rather have him near, in Celatas, but how he serves—or if he serves—is for him to decide."

"And me! I am going to demand a long honeymoon before any decision."

"And well you should. What say you to a wedding at the Feast of Flowers? With royal hosting."

Three weeks? Well, a little more but still too soon! "Maybe Summer Feast would be better." She knew she sounded tentative.

"Maybe so. It would allow you some time to prepare. Not to mention Blen."

Blen would probably wed her tomorrow, given the choice. "I'll ask him." That was the most sensible thing.

"Now," spoke the king, "how soon will you be ready to ride in the morn?"

~ ~ ~

"Trade does come across these hills," said Donzalo, "but there is no real road down to my uncle's keep. It would benefit everyone if there were."

From the walls they could see the path they had followed up here from Paren's manor. No more than a dirt track through the valley, not passable by wagons. They were not far from a real road, however, and the crossroads where Donzalo had first met her brother.

"Better to learn the roads already here," she told him.

Oder was gone and there was no knowing when he might return. He traveled to the distant capital of the Anian Empire, perhaps to receive new honors and new duties. Ansa knew she would never glimpse its spires and domes again, rising before the towering back-drop of the Gocan Mountains, the range sacred to Father Sky. Their existence was barely a rumor here, where they were oft named the Lofty Mountains.

"Yes," agreed her husband. "It is certain a good road crosses into Lama somewhere south of River Abam."

Or perhaps Oder would choose to retire to their ancestral lands, an expanse of steppe with far more sheep and cattle than men. She had ridden free over those lands when young, and along the shores of the great inland sea, Coyas.

Yes, most would name it a lake. But Ansa had never seen a real sea until she left her home. Many things she had not seen.

"Have you noticed the little people about?" Ansa asked of a sudden. The thought had just found its way into her head.

"Others. Yes, I have. Keeping an eye on us." He gazed out over the countryside, maybe hoping to spy one. "I met a queen of kobolds once. When I dreamed in the caverns of the fay."

"You've never spoken much of that. I learned more about the place from Fachalana."

"There was pain in my memories of that time."

"No more?"

"I am at peace with them now." One more long look at the land

195

around the keep, their land, before turning to her. "I may have needed to find love to fully be healed."

Maybe that was true of all of us, thought Ansa.

~ ~ ~

"The Feast of Flowers could be cutting things close. A delay of some sort could prevent us even reaching the capital by then."

She snuggled closer to him. "Let's do it right now."

"I'd rather not get out of bed."

"Idiot. I meant in the morning, before we leave. There's a priest somewhere in this place."

There was a long silence in the dark. What was he thinking? "Do not cheat the king of this, Fachalana. I think he sees you almost as a daughter."

Oh, Blen *was* the sort to bring up ideas about duty and all that. "Then I'll tell him a Feast of Flowers wedding is on. He can send messengers ahead to set it all up, so we needn't be there till the day!"

And there was no one much she could think of inviting. That could be left to the king's functionaries as well. Or Lady Lis. She was likely to take charge. "But," she told her husband-to-be, "if we find ourselves still on the road, we will stop at the closest temple and marry there."

"Agreed."

That was settled. Now for— "Mmm, yes."

~ ~ ~

Captain Habidros's chest was swelling with pride nearly as much as his wife's belly was with their child. Orgelo looked at his son over his goblet rim. "If you don't settle down and marry soon, Lanesha's offspring may become my heir."

"Good," said Sorsen. "That lets me off the hook!"

196

His son exasperated him, preferring to ride with his lancers to attending to his duties as the next count. It wasn't that the boy disliked women. There had been plenty of evidence otherwise! But choosing one to marry seemed too difficult a chore.

"Oh, you know I'll do it one of these days," Sorsen assured his father. "But it does make it less pressing, doesn't it?"

Count Orgelo had to admit that was true. Not that he would say so aloud. "The brother of Habidros is back in our area," he said.

"Galaro, yes. I've had men keeping an eye on him and his traders though they haven't actually crossed the border."

He might have let him know of it sooner. The count had only been informed this day.

"Looks like he's going toward the coast. A rendezvous with one of his suppliers, I'd guess."

"We're likely to see him coming back then." Orgelo was likely to see a cut on the goods the trader carried through his county. That was nothing to complain about.

"You know Lady Aldea has a daughter of marriageable age," he said. "Maybe you should pay her a visit."

"Aldea?"

"Donzalo's aunt, sister to Borrago. She and Sir Moros have a nice place in County Ivosam." Or so he had heard.

"Kind of far."

"My boy, it is always best when one's in-laws live far away."

"Ha, then maybe I should seek a wife in Sharsh!"

Anywhere, said Orgelo, again only to himself.

7

THE WAGON HAD been sent ahead a day earlier. Not the cart with which they arrived, but another. They need not hold themselves to its speed.

In truth, they rushed toward Celatas, King Lareth being as eager to reach it as Fachalana and Blen. Doufan and Godos were not nearly so pleased with being forced to hurry.

They did pass their luggage by within a short time.

"I've never been on this road before," Godos informed the ambassador. The two oft found themselves riding together. "Nor in the mountains much at all."

"Your family does not pack themselves off to them as soon as it grows a bit warm in Celatas? It seems all those with the means desert the city."

"No, Dad takes us to the coast instead. His idea of a vacation is to visit all his ships!" His eyes swept the forested slopes. "But I like visiting these tall trees."

"Which Fornos Tasetha would like to turn into masts, no doubt."

"Indeed so, my lord! It seems you know him."

Doufan smiled, but only slightly. "We are acquainted."

Godos barely noticed. His mind was filling with things he wanted to say, things he hadn't been able to express before. "I used to think his religion made him so, but the Kamatians of Lama aren't like him at all."

"Not those of the south, where you were. You'll find it different elsewhere."

"Oh. You have traveled an awful lot, haven't you? But then, so has my father."

"Some take themselves to the world. Some take their world with them."

"Oh, that's a good one, sir."

"And believe it or not, I just made it up. I think this fellow wishes to speak with me."

He did not. One of the Lareth's attendants had ridden back to them, but it was for another than Lord Doufan he carried a message. "The king asks you to ride with him, young sir," he told Godos.

One did as a king requested, no matter how nervous. Fachalana and Blen were with the monarch; a little support from them would help.

"All the Nafals should be invited," Lady Fachalana was saying. A man was scribbling this down as they rode.

"There are quite a few of them, my dear," the king told her. "But be it so. Any more?"

"No, my lord, that should do."

The king himself took the paper, made his mark on it, folded it over and handed it to a courier. "Ride to Celatas, and quickly."

It took little time for man and horse to vanish around a corner ahead. To Godos's consternation, Blen and Fachalana also vanished, dropping back, leaving him with Lareth. He waited for the king to address him. Maybe he would forget he was there!

"Our Doufan tells me you are quite a dunderhead. He says also you have promise."

"I have heard the first of those from my father, your highness."

"Most sons do. I have heard worse of you over the years. And there was that business with my own son."

Which one did he mean?

"You know, your connection to both Prince Gawis and the would-be assassin of Modareth led some to believe one of my sons wished the other dead."

"I—I never heard that before, my lord." Nor thought of it. But he should have!

199

"Your father wisely sent you off to sea before the rumors swirled. I've heard interesting things of your adventures, lad. Tell me the story."

"Yes, your highness." Talking to a king wasn't so hard after all, was it?

~ ~ ~

"Sir Paren should spend more time here. He needs to be visible so the people of County Rosam don't think a pair of foreigners are running everything."

"But we are." Lomela told him. "And you know there is another Rosam who can be seen."

"Another?" She didn't mean Donzalo, surely. Though he would love to see him here.

"The Count Ros himself. I think I should take him riding with me."

"He is admittedly better looking than Paren."

"He's the handsomest little lad in the world. Traspa told me so."

"It is an excellent idea. He's not big enough to sit a pony yet." Jobareth was fairly certain of that.

He could accuse his lady love of snickering at him. "Give him a year at least! I'll carry him before me until then. That will look good." She turned to pick up a letter from her desk. "Sir Sorsen wrote me. He has the most dreadful spelling, nearly as bad as Fachalana."

"He doesn't hope to woo you from me, does he?" He wouldn't put it past the man. Sorsen and Orgelo alike would love such an alliance with County Rosam.

"Fear not, my Jobo. He asks about Donzalo's cousin, a girl who lives up the river somewhere." She scanned the page. "County Ivosam."

"Across Weldar and a bit north. Small."

"Well, Donzalo's Aunt, um, Aldea married a brother of the current count and they have a daughter of a proper age. Sorsen, in his clumsy way, suggests we invite her here so he can visit on neutral ground, so to speak."

"In other words, so he can check her out without dealing with her parents."

"Just the way you men think. I am going to send an invite. It would be good to know the relatives." She took a fresh sheet of paper, dipped her pen. "But I might inconvenience Sorsen by inviting her mother too."

It sounded good to Jobareth Nafal. It would be another Rosam to show the populace, as well.

~ ~ ~

At last the King's Road joined the River Chas, wide but no longer swollen with the spring floods. They would parallel its course into the capital.

"It seems you're not to be late for your wedding," remarked Godos.

"We can still disinvite you, you know," Fachalana told him. "Does your father own any of those boats?"

Quite a few floated on the Chas, going both directions. "Nope. We don't operate anything above the bridge. Different licensing."

"Too much expense?"

"Not legal. The laws don't allow one operator to hold both upper river and lower river permits. It's supposed to prevent unfair advantages or something."

Blen spoke. "I am sure there are those who find ways around that."

"They try. There are hefty fines *and* the loss of all licenses if they're caught." His voice lowered, as if conveying a confidence. "Dad has turned in a few cheats."

"Good for him," said the knight. He had perhaps a little too much respect for the law.

Godos grinned. "Good for business too."

It was fortuitous when morality and profit managed to dovetail, felt Fachalana. The problems came when one attempted to force that morality to fit. It sometimes took a rather large hammer.

Buildings grew closer together with every mile they traveled. Warehouses, inns. Shanties further back from the road and water. Soon they were in the outskirts of Celatas, approaching the city gates. The gates didn't actually keep anyone out, not being attached to a wall; soldiers looked over those who passed them, occasionally stopping someone from boredom to check credentials.

No one stopped the king. Through they rode. There was the King's Bridge downriver and villas dotted the slopes to their left, above the city streets and stench. Above all stood Lareth's keep.

"Are you going home now or coming with us?" Fachalana asked Godos. It was already understood that she and Blen would stay with the king until after the wedding. She had no idea of Doufan's inten-tions nor did she intend to ask.

"Do you think I'd pass up being able to stay in the castle?" asked the boy.

So all turned aside at the road that led up to it. "Your villa," Doufan whispered as they passed the way leading to the low house, hidden among trees and bushes. Radal had insisted on having growing things around the place. They looked neglected.

"And mine. I leave you now, my friends," said the diplomat, and he turned aside, alone. His scribe was still far behind them with the luggage.

"I spent a good amount of my childhood running about this place," she told Blen, as they approached the wide main gate, with its pointed arch of tawny stone. Carved figures of the gods stood on either side.

"I've never been here."

"I'll show you all the best places to conceal yourself if we play hide-and-seek."

"I would never hide myself from you."

And so they passed on into the castle of the king of Sharsh.

8

HE HAD PUT it off long enough. His parents would know he was here. Godos strolled out of King Lareth's castle into the mid-morning sun. Not by the main gate; there were many ways out. Whether they would prove ways in, he wasn't sure.

There was no reason he couldn't visit here again though, was there? He was the close personal friend of Lady Fachalana, after all! His house was over that way. Close enough to readily walk. Yes, he could even see its roofs from here, the pale slate catching the morning light, but the roadway between them wound around the hillside.

That was fine with him. He was in no hurry. Who owned that house? Grandiose. Probably a noble. Oh, there was the Nafals' sprawling but unassuming villa. He'd have to visit. He'd promised. A guard looked him over as he passed. It was suspicious for anyone to be walking here.

And his own home, the Tasetha villa. The sturdy iron gates were closed and locked. Still? Godos realized he had no idea when they were normally opened. In recent years, he had generally been asleep at this time of morning. Well, no problem. He'd climbed over them many a time, but usually at night!

"Hold there," a voice growled, as he dropped on the other side. "Oh, Master Godos! You could have hollered, sir, and I'd 've let you in."

"This is more fun," he informed the fellow. One of the gardeners. He grinned. "As long as someone doesn't bash me with a spade."

The man lowered the one he carried. "It's good to see you back, sir."

Which probably wasn't true. "It's not so bad being back." But he wasn't convinced he wanted to be. Up the wide walkway to the front doors. He might as well make a grand entrance there.

No, he wasn't going to get the chance. His parents were spoiling it all by coming out to greet him. Each he embraced in turn before anyone spoke.

"We expected you yesterday," said his father.

"I was the king's guest." That was an answer with which no one could reasonably argue.

But his father did. "King Lareth invited you to stay with him?" There was more than a little doubt in his voice.

"More Lady Fachalana, truly. Lareth may not have even known I stayed," he admitted. "But I have got to know the king. We've had long conversations. Honest!" It sounded preposterous even to him.

"That," said his mother, "must be why we received an invitation to the viscountess' wedding."

"She'll expect a gift, I suppose," grumbled Fronos. "Well, let's get inside."

"Do you know the groom too?"

"Yes, Mom. We rode together all the way from the other side of Lama."

"Lama. You'll have to tell me all about your time there."

"Let's feed the boy first."

"Excellent idea! It's a goodly walk from Lareth's keep and I've built up quite an appetite!"

A long story it was. Longer than Godos had anticipated when he started its telling. And there were plenty enough interruptions and questions from both parents, and the whole thing ran on into a second meal.

"This Galaro," said his father. "In what sort of merchandise does he deal?"

"Weapons are his specialty, Dad, but he'll buy and sell anything.

The gunnes are mostly from Lorj. He says the craftsmen there are every bit as good as ours in Sharsh."

"I would agree. But not the equal to the best from the Siphic cities."

Godos nodded. Galaro had said much the same. "Most of our trade was in legal goods. And what wasn't legal was smuggled mostly to avoid customs."

"Our?" asked his mother.

"I was a member of the troop. Well, not really. Just a hireling, in fact. Oh, by the way I owe Galaro for buying me from those smugglers."

"And what else did he buy from them?"

"Oh, this and that. Muram lace. It's a roundabout way to get it there but apparently the others are worse."

His father nodded now. He was likely to understand that.

"Silk and brandy are more likely to go the other way. Pearls! Pearls from the southern isles, and jewelry and fine workmanship of all sorts."

Fronos Tasetha pondered his son. "It seems you enjoy trade," he said.

"Yep. Surprising isn't it?"

"You've no idea."

~ ~ ~

Blen was not really a mean swordsman. He could readily defeat nine of any ten men he might face. She would have to take on the tenth, it seemed.

Fencing with him—fencing with anyone—was a good way to calm her nerves these last few days before the wedding. She didn't care about the damned dress and the flowers and all the other decisions people thought they should bring to her. Go ask someone else! Go ask Lady Lis!

Was this another one coming? Oh! "Lord Doufan. It is good to see you again." The man ambled across the courtyard, in a long, softly draping blue tunic, edged with fur.

"Have you come to take my place, sir?" asked Blen.

"I know better than to cross swords with the lady," he answered. "I wished to let you know our baggage cart arrived this morn. I have already carried my scribe's sheet of lettering to Nafal's printer friend. His shop is most interesting." Then a congenial smile. "And my scribe himself is resting in my villa, vowing never again to travel."

"And will you travel no more, my lord?"

"Who can say? I've no desire today but next month, next year—I might if the king were to ask."

"I want to go see where Blen grew up," declared Fachalana. "I looked at a map and it's not so far from my own country estate."

"A honeymoon journey. An excellent idea, my lady. Will you also be visiting your villa here?"

"Not until after the wedding. Maybe not until after the honeymoon!"

"Quite understandable. There were a few things of your father's in the wagon. The king says he will hold them until you are ready to deal with them."

The cask. That too would wait. Maybe forever. "I thank you, sir. Now perhaps you can point out this fellow's mistakes to him."

Doufan bowed. "Your only mistake, my dear Blen, is crossing swords with the lady when you should be kissing her."

It was pretty good advice, wasn't it?

~ ~ ~

"We brought this traveler over too," said the smuggler, nodding toward a cloaked figure.

"I don't want to know about that," Galaro growled. "If you help someone slip across the strait, that's your business and his. But—" His scowl deepened further. "If you bring them against their will, you'll answer to me. I'll have no slaving."

"That trade was played out long ago on these coasts. Even girls for whore houses." The man scratched at his beard, furrowed his brow. "'Cept maybe in Morparas. I keep my distance from Morparas."

"That is wisdom. Let's see these gunnes. Ah." All wheel-locks, all pistols. The sort of thing he wanted to see. Galaro could make no profit on a match-lock musket. "Pretty enough, but do they shoot well?"

"Some," opined the smuggler, "care more how their gunnes look than how they work."

"And I'm not one of them, as you know. I've a reputation for quality merchandise."

"Reckon you'll have to try them out." The fellow grinned at him. "As usual."

Galaro did, methodically, one after the other, firing at a fallen tree. The smugglers' mysterious passenger sat and watched, saying nothing.

"Sound enough," he admitted. "Mechanically. As to their accuracy, I'm not impressed."

Not that he'd expected much but he needed a bargaining point. And a bargain was made, on this and sundry other goods. It was then the cloaked stranger approached.

A woman. "I need to travel north," she said without preamble. "I would pay good gold to ride with you."

The accent was of the colorless sort affected by some travelers, one that revealed little of her origins. "I could take your gold and leave you somewhere along our road. And not necessarily alive."

"You have a reputation for more than quality merchandise, Sir Galaro. You're known for fair dealing." There was a quick smile. "Albeit sharp dealing."

He had no real reason not to take her gold. One woman would not inconvenience them. "Would Tod-ford suit you?" he asked.

"It would very well. Would two Crowns suit you?"

He would not have asked that much even before dealing. "It will. One now, in good faith, the other when we get there."

She handed over the large coin, stamped with the image of a fiery eagle above a coronet.

"You can ride in the wagon," he said, and returned to his preparations. Half an hour later they were heading back toward the north. To Lama and another season of trading.

~ ~ ~

There was no hope of seeing Lady Fachalana before the wedding. Two days away! And after that? She and her handsome husband might ride off somewhere at once.

Handsome he was. Erlana had seen him at the theater last night, with Fachalana and Prince Modareth. Not Sir Pol. He was handsome too. But different. She gazed out the window. She didn't feel like writing or anything else.

One of the maids entered the salon. "There is a caller," she announced. "A Master Tasetha."

Oh, what a bother! "Do bring him in," said her mother.

Godos. She didn't remember him so tanned! He'd always seemed to have a sickly pallor in the old days. No surprise for a man who slept most of the day and spent the nights in taverns. Still rather ugly though, with his snub nose. He looked like her mother's lapdog!

But—wouldn't he be a great source of ideas for the play? She had admittedly run dry of them.

"My son tells me you have become friends. Do sit down and tell us how you met. Erlana, will you run to the kitchen and remind them to bring refreshments? Now Master Godos. Was Jobareth well when last you saw him?"

She'd let Mom pump him for stories now. But she'd get her turn! And he might even help her in seeing Lady Fachalana. Erlana was feeling better about Godos Tasetha with every step, as she hurried down the hall.

But he was still homely. That she was not going to deny.

9

"The form of Asak seen here was not his true form, his form in his own world, but a manifestation. There was as much of the sorcerer Radal to it as there was of the god."

"Just as Nosana's black cat was not Dekata's true shape," said Jobareth.

"So I would think." Grippo grinned. "Of course, you never saw that, just as I never saw what went on here that night."

Jobareth Nafal enjoyed these discussions with the Kamatian novice. They had been having them, off and on, for more than a year. Two years, this fall. "You do not believe Asak is the ultimate evil."

"I'll admit that here, with you. Nowhere else." Not if he hoped to be ordained. "I believe the god aspires to it, but he can never become the infinite void."

"We all aspire," said Jobareth. "None ever succeed completely."

"Exactly! This god of evil, Asak, wants to commit suicide and take all existence with him. Completely impossible, as existence is infinite too."

"But he can still destroy and ruin."

"He and those who follow him, knowingly or not. Ultimately, they too hate existence."

"But they can't kill God. Who I suppose you might say both is and isn't Kamat."

"Something like that."

"Did you know Lord Doufan is a Munuan?"

"Really? I wish I'd known so I could speak with him of it."

"He would not have. Doufan is exceedingly private about some things."

Grippo refilled his goblet before asking, "Then how do you know?"

"His scribe let it slip. He follows the ways of munu too."

"Some Partanacans are Munuans."

"More are Kamatians, including the imperial family. I think the scribe is Coradean, not Partanacan. Whichever, he does hail from Lorj. Where I would guess Doufan learned of the Munuan way." The man had spent time there; that Jobareth had also learned from his secretary. "They don't quite believe in evil, do they?"

"They might think it's an illusion or something like that. But they believe one can lack munu and that sounds somewhat the same to me."

"A force that fills all things. That's probably not at all a good way to put it."

"Munuans say there is no good way to put it, except to call it munu."

"It's easier to stick with the old gods. At least they show themselves now and again. They act."

"But even they know there is something higher than themselves."

"Oh? Maybe there are atheist gods."

"That is a disturbing thought, my friend. Is this the wine your family sent? It is—I'm not sure of the word. Maybe better than any I've ever had."

"As indescribable as munu." Both chuckled over that. Having had several glasses of the vintage may have made it seem funnier than it was. "My old friend Pol, that country boy I took under my wing, is now advising Prince Modareth what sort of wine to purchase."

"He should tell him to buy some of this."

"Probably has. This is a fine Arolin wine and Pol is an Arolinian himshelf—himself. He claims all the best wines come from there."

"And do they?"

"The best come from Arolin when one is selling an Arolin wine. And the best come from Dor when one sells a wine of Dor. This I learned from growing up with a family of wine sellers."

"And the wine one is drinking right now," said Grippo, raising his glass, "is always the best of all."

~ ~ ~

"Arlacas has traditionally been a part of Sharsh, our outlet to the Lesser Sea. The port is in Coradean hands now."

"And that continues to be a point of contention," spoke Prince Gawis.

"That it does," agreed his brother. "The Imperial Union, as some are referring to it now, would make it even more difficult for Sharsh to ever reclaim the city."

"Uh-huh." These were all things he knew. "There used to be a canal down there, didn't there?"

Modareth for once looked uncertain about an historical point. "I seem to remember—something." He went to his bookshelves, chose a volume. "No, no," he muttered. Another. "Yes, here it is. It ran down through the swamps from the Chas to the Arlac."

"That would be useful."

"It undoubtedly was. Built before the Ani invaded and fell into disrepair after."

"Maybe whoever ends up owning Arlacas might want to cooperate on reopening it." Gawis chuckled. "It is likely our father has thought of that."

"You should mention it to him anyway." Modareth had returned to his chair, but was still holding the book open. There was a map of the canal route on the parchment page.

"I shall. Ah, Father is rather big on the man Lady Fachalana is going to marry."

"It seems he has been for some time. He had plans for Sir Blen. Has plans for him."

"I doubt they included Fachalana." He spoke jestingly, maybe even the slightest sarcastically, but Modareth ignored it and gave him a serious reply.

"He fully approves of the match now. That I know." A pause for another thought on it. "Tomorrow's wedding is evidence of that."

The wedding his father was taking pains over, the wedding of a common soldier and the daughter of a traitor.

"Sir Blen and the Viscountess Fachalana may be a couple to reckon with," finished Modareth.

Indeed they might. But how best to reckon with them? Gawis rose. "I'm for my own chambers. I'll see you tomorrow."

~ ~ ~

Radal did not have her narrower, higher nose, thought Lareth, and more resembled his father, who was dark even for a Lorjam. As dark as the Princess Mara.

If Fachalana looked like anyone, it was her paternal grandmother, the woman driven mad by her unrecognized powers, the woman who had thrown herself from a tower window. That had hurt both husband and son; Ildor had died in battle not so long after. Some said he took unnecessary risks.

Could Radal's descent have begun at the same time? The king did not know. The changes in his friend were unmistakable, looking back, but imperceptible from day to day, year to year.

Decade to decade. They should have grown old together, sitting before the hearth with their memories.

He rather wished he could have walked her to the priest. Not one person thought it a good idea. Doufan would do. Doufan was a good man and had become a friend to Lady Fachalana. To her soon-to-be husband, as well.

He must decide how to use both men. Blen stood before the table, where the marriage agreement would be signed. That took place before the high priest of Jov stepped forward and performed his ceremony. Prince Modareth at his side. Fachalana had surely asked his son to stand with him.

He'd rather have Sir Blen friendly with his other son. He was just the sort of man Gawis would need. Here came Lord Doufan and the bride. This sunny morning was excellent for a wedding, wasn't it?

He should certainly name Doufan to his council. Chief Coun-cilor? Maybe not; that was more a ceremonial post anyway. Radal had never worn the title, even though he had dominated the council. Doufan remained best utilized behind the scenes. As Radal, he might well become Lareth's closest advisor.

Maybe I should appoint a woman to the council, mused Lareth. It had been done before, hadn't it? Back in the days before his dynasty ruled Sharsh. Neither of his daughters-in-law. They were good women both—and knowledgeable—but neither was assertive enough. Best their advice remain behind the scenes too.

If only he could appoint Radal's daughter! It would take some time before she was accepted and, then, she might not wish such a role. The marriage contract signed and witnessed, the Chief Scribe of Sharsh stepped away, the Chief Priest stepped forward. There were both those daughters-in-law, attentive on the words of the cere-mony, both with babies in their arms. Neither was the sort to hand their infant off to a nursemaid.

And all over. On to a reception and the boredom of listening to the small talk of his nobles through a long afternoon.

10

"Riders, Captain!"

He looked where the trader pointed. Yes, two horsemen, keeping their distance but obviously interested in their caravan. There was no telling who they might be—chance-met travelers or scouts for bandits.

"Keep moving," ordered Galaro.

Most of the traders, all his old troop, had mustered south of Orgelo's borders. That rendezvous spot they had used for years. It had been far too late to get to Tod-ford by the Feast of Flowers nor had they particularly intended to. May Festival they were more inclined to call it here in the south. Was it today or yesterday?

Some years they would have bypassed Orgelo's place altogether on their journey north and not seen it until late summer, at the Feast of Plenty. That had become a regular stop and, sometimes, the winding up of the season for those who preferred not to travel in autumn and winter. Best he let the count see his merchandise this year, aye, and pay a fee for bringing it through County Arvaram. Slipping past now would only create later ill will.

The riders were vanished. They'd be advised to keep a lookout for trouble anyway. All the traders went armed, gunnes, swords. Galaro's eye went to their guest, the woman perched on the back of one of the wagons, legs hanging over. He hadn't been able to keep from noticing she carried not one but two small pistols concealed about her.

He would not be at all surprised were there a knife as well. She hadn't even given him her name, nor had he asked. She would only provide a false one. No matter, she'd leave them at Tod-ford. They might reach it by tomorrow evening.

"Ho! Don't string out so!" he called to the column, nodding to the woman as he rode past.

~ ~ ~

"My wife—" That sounded so good! "My wife insisted my family be invited, though it was doubtful any could come. At such short a notice."

"At least they know you got married," said Fachalana. "You wouldn't even have told them."

"They haven't heard anything of me in a decade, my wife." He wanted to keep saying that. "And it is likely they have only the vaguest idea of who you are."

"They'll find out. We *are* going to visit them."

"On your honeymoon, my lady?" asked Doufal.

"Yes, if we can decide when that will be. You know, our child-hood homes were not so far apart, across the hills from each other."

"I on the Chas and she on the Indor," added Blen. That hadn't been necessary, he told himself. Doufan would have known.

"But I would have still been a skinny little girl when you were growing into manhood."

"I had barely begun to when I ran off to join the army. I have what, three or four years of age on you at most?"

"I suppose." She seemed thoughtful of a sudden. Totting up their age difference? No, it proved something else. "You ran away? That seems rather impetuous, my Blen, and not at all in character for you."

"I thought on it quite a long time first."

"I can imagine," commented Doufan. "I'd best go be seen by other people here. And other people definitely want to see you." He gave them a bow. "My lord and lady."

Blen watched him pass into the crowd, a word or greeting here and there. "Am I supposed to be called 'lord' now?" he asked his wife.

"I'm not really sure! Do you want me to call you that?"

"I'll expect it from now on." He also expected his wife's snicker. "That one young lady has been staring at us for some time," he said.

"Should that be surprising today? But alas, our fame will fade too soon!" Fachalana sighed dramatically. "Ha, I'm as much a ham as ever! Which young lady?"

"Over there." He hoped his nod was sufficient. He wasn't going to start pointing at people.

"Oh. That's Jobareth's sister. We should speak to her later, when we have time. And definitely invite her to visit."

"It might be simpler to drop by the Nafals' house."

"Only if you want to talk about wine all night."

~ ~ ~

"Throw out big stupid man. You live in tower!" stated the kobold.

"Not so easily done," Vis told him. A handful of other little people crowded behind him. More kobolds, a troll. She thought that bigger one was some sort of ogre. "Donzalo is a more than competent knight. His wife is a fighting woman, too, I'm told."

"Eat her!" one of the Others called out. "Yummy!"

She hoped they didn't harbor similar intentions toward her. Maybe deprivations of late had made her too bony.

"I'm not sure the people around here would accept me anyway. They seem to like their new laird. When Sabatare came the tower stood abandoned."

"Sabatare. Pah!" spoke the kobold. "Always think bigger wizard than he was."

"It got him killed," added the troll, who seemed to speak the Muram better than the others. She hadn't tried Krevod on them. It didn't seem so common down here as in the Upper Cuddon.

The kobold nodded, his long pointed nose bobbing up and down.

"Bad man kill bad man. We part battle over way." He gestured west or maybe northwest. "Stupid we. Stay away from big people fights now."

Vis actually knew a little, albeit at third or fourth hand, of the battle in which the wizard had perished. Lord Radal's frustrated henchman Sojel had put a sword into him when he saw they had lost.

"So," she asked, "how do you propose we make ourselves owner of the keep? You say you're staying away from fights now."

"Pester them. Mischief do!"

"Maybe they'll get sick of it and leave," said the troll. His little gray face betrayed his doubt of this.

Maybe she could do a little mischief too. Vis still knew some tricks.

~ ~ ~

They chose a good place for it. The attackers were not numerous but they were well-horsed and well-armed, and had concealed them-selves in a little copse by one of shallow streams singing its way down to the Tod. A volley from their pistols and then they were among them, swords drawn and slashing.

But not, seemingly, intent on killing. Not unless someone stood in their way. Straight toward the wagon with the nameless woman they bore. She rose and cooly discharged both her gunnes at the attackers, then stood ready with sword in hand. Where had she gotten that?

"Take her," cried out one, probably their leader. "Alive if you can!"

It was somewhat obvious she did not intend to allow that. Galaro spurred toward her, his own pistols in each hand, his reins barely retained by his fingertips. Others were rallying after the first shock of the attack but seemed uncertain of what was going on. The riders

219

seemed intent on keeping them confused, galloping back and forth, crying out. None had discharged another gunne.

These traders of his were veterans of the road. They'd get straightened out in a moment. Galaro fired one gunne, the other, and then crashed into the closest horseman, his saber already in hand. Then someone crashed into him, hands pulled him from the saddle, and he lay flat on the grass as the melee continued about him.

Good way to get stomped. He instinctively rolled to the cover of the closest wagon, to look out and spy their guest being taken, hauled down and thrown across a saddle before one of the men. Damned if he'd allow this!

And she still owed him a crown. He came out with his only weapon left, a long knife. Other traders were exchanging blows with the intruders, slashing, parrying, but it appeared they were preparing to retreat.

The sound of more hooves, many hooves. The horsemen turned, began to ride, but Galaro leaped upon the one bearing away the captive. A moment latter, two men and a woman sprawled on the ground. Only two rose, for the one man's throat was cut.

"You jump rather well for a large man," the woman told him.

"Yes, and despite getting old and fat," came a cheerful, familiar voice. "Well met, Brother."

"Well met indeed, Habi. Well met indeed."

11

OH, SIR POL was going to give them something! Erlana had been thoroughly bored by the two poets who preceded him, with long-winded and pointless blatherings on the sanctity of marriage and the joy of the people and the blessings of the gods and so on. It certainly wasn't as good as her brother's stuff!

Maybe it wasn't even as good as her stuff, though she dismissed that thought at once. Pol stepped onto the low platform, gave the newlyweds a graceful bow. Wasn't that gray tunic a little too somber for a wedding? A spring wedding, at that.

"I wrote this with you two in mind," announced the boyish poet, "but I'll leave it to you decide which is speaking."

> I've nothing in common with you, my dear,
> nothing in common at all;
> You are the blithe springtime of the year
> and I the cold wind of fall.
>
> I've nothing in common with you, I fear,
> for as you may well recall,
> I'd far rather sit and drink my beer
> while you yearn to dance at the ball.
>
> I've nothing in common with you, and here
> most likely is what would befall
> if we were to whisper in a friend's ear—
> you'd charm and I would appall.

I've nothing in common with you, it's clear,
the differences are not small;
indeed, I am inclined to cheer
at moments when you might bawl!

I've nothing in common with you, the mere
thought of you, perfect and tall
reminds me wherever I might appear,
folks tell me I make their skin crawl.

I've nothing in common with you, my dear,
and yet I long for your call;
no, nothing in common with you, my dear,
nothing in common at all.

Well, Fachalana certainly loved it! And Blen was laughing too. It took the rest of the crowd a few seconds. Oh, Princess Carana was practically on the floor with mirth, while her husband at least looked amused.

Prince Gawis was whispering in the ear of a baffled Mara, perhaps trying to explain it. That was when Sir Pol suddenly cried out, staring toward the right of the royal couple, and Fachalana sprang from her seat.

A man—a figure anyway—in a dark caftan moved directly toward the crown prince and his wife, holding a dirk. The viscountess might not have been the closest a second ago but she was now, and a knife had appeared in her own hand. Pol had hopped down and was close behind.

"Stay, sir!" she yelled at the intruder. More were up and moving now, including Prince Gawis.

The man didn't even seem to see her. His face was expressionless.

Blank. The eyes didn't even seem to focus but Erlana was not nearly close enough to be sure. Fachalana's knife went into his chest. Well, he'd had plenty of warning.

He did not stop but pushed her aside. Astonished, perhaps, and certainly unprepared, Fachalana tripped backward, crashing into Pol and sending both to the ground. The man moved forward—not toward Gawis who had stepped out with his own dagger but dodging around him toward the princess and her baby.

That was when someone leaped on his back and bore him to the ground. Guards were soon around and helped the hero to his feet. Why it was Godos! Erlana pushed forward, though she had no good reason. She did so want to know what was going on.

"Why, he's dead, sir," said one soldier.

"Smells like he's been dead for some time," said another, backing away a little.

Gawis seemed to concur. He certainly got no closer. Fachalana, however, had to get down and examine the body, stench or no, Pol on one side and her new husband on the other. She could not hear what they whispered to each other.

Here came the king. "What happened? Doufan and I were sharing a drink in the tent."

"An assassin, sir," said Gawis.

"After you?" He looked over the body, took a step closer, wrinkled his nose, took a step back.

You can smell it, can't you? Erlana said to herself. Her desire to know more outweighed her desire for clean air, at least for the moment.

"It seems certain his wife or son was the target, not the prince," Fachalana said, rising. "He—it—might have gotten to them too, were it not for Godos."

Lareth might not have expected that but he did not seem surprised either. "How did you happen to be close, boy?"

"Um, your highness, you see I got up there—" He pointed out the knee-high base of a nearby column. "So I could see and hear a little better but what I did see was this, um, man come by, walking all stiff and unnatural. Then everything happened all at once and I jumped on him and—well, that's pretty much it."

Prince Gawis gave him a close look for the first time. "I say, Godos! I haven't seen you in ages. When did you get back?"

"Last week, my lord."

Pol had risen too. "I think that is a fitting conclusion to our entertainment, don't you? Let us allow the newlyweds to go their way and the rest of us get out of here."

Sir Blen and Lady Fachalana appeared to agree. More importantly, so did the king. Erlana joined her family as they left the colonnaded courtyard, an enclosed lawn just outside the castle walls frequently used for such events.

Godos Tesetha, a hero. Who would ever have thought it?

~ ~ ~

"We'd had word of armed men on the border and Orgelo sent me to take a look."

"Not Sorsen?" To be sure, Galaro would rather see his brother than the count's son

"He's gone off courting. Some girl who's visiting at Castle Rosam."

There had been damage, and a man dead. The traders had done what they could here; they'd attend to the rest when they reached Tod-ford. It looked like there'd be a longer stay than anticipated.

Galaro gave a long look to the woman who had been the target of the raid, again seated in the back of a wagon, as if all was as before.

He would need to have a long talk with her. Or maybe just collect his payment at Tod-ford and say good riddance. He had no need to know who or what she was.

Not that he couldn't guess. A spy out of Sharsh, who'd gotten into trouble down in Lorj. Big trouble considering the men they'd sent after her. She should have let him know there was danger. His dead trader was on her. Yes, he decided, he would demand another Crown for the man's family.

"So, Habi, how is the wife doing?"

~ ~ ~

Fachalana had not wanted to return to magic this soon. Magic of any sort. But that night, as Blen slept, she called out.

To the Partanacan sorcerer Axacles she called.

Lady Fachalana. How did you know I wouldn't be sleeping?

I suspected you were the sort to take a long siesta and then stay awake into the wee hours.

He laughed a deep laugh. *So it is. I must admit, your call is a surprise.* If he was nervous—which was likely—he hid it well.

There was an attempted assassination of the Princess Mara today. Or maybe her son. No need to say that.

Mara? He actually seemed outraged. *Coradean terrorists!* he hissed.

Coradeans?

Who seek to prevent the union of the empires. To disrupt what has been achieved so far.

Hmm, that's possible. I could see the daughter of the emperor being a target. She would mention it to Lareth, anyway. *The would-be assassin was a walking corpse, reanimated in some way.*

Ah. Axacles remained silent.

Could the Coradeans do this?

225

I do not know, my Lady. I have not the skills to create such an abomination, nor the stomach. Few do.

But you know how it is done?

I do. The sorcerer sends a part of himself around through another world to enter the corpse. To become one with it and control it. This is exceedingly dangerous. One might become trapped there if it—deteriorates too much while one is linked.

I think only a madman would do such a thing. A very powerful madman. She had someone in mind but would not name him to this man. *But why he would I can not understand.*

For some, Axacles said softly, *doing evil is reason enough in itself.*

Perhaps he did suspect the same man as she. *I thank you, Axacles, for daring to speak with me.*

For now, my lady, we may well be on the same side of things.

Both broke away in unspoken agreement. Fachalana slipped into bed beside her husband. "Humm?" he said.

"Duty called," she whispered and snuggled close.

12

"WE RAN INTO a little trouble, my lord. My brother came along to help, not that we really needed him."

"They weren't bandits," Habidros added, ignoring his brother's assertion. "Looked to be after that woman over there."

All three turned their eyes to her. A demure, nondescript little thing, she seemed. "A spy?"

Galaro had not been going to suggest that to Count Orgelo. The man's unfriendliness to Sharsh and Sharshites was no secret. There was no telling how he might treat a suspected Sharshite spy. "Perhaps," he admitted, and then told the nobleman the whole of his experience with her.

"And you don't even know her name?"

"She would have given a false one."

"That's better than calling her 'the woman' as you seem to have been." Orgelo motioned her to to come to them. "What should I name you, mistress?" he asked.

"Bela, my lord."

An exceedingly common name, and not just in Sharsh. "Do you carry papers for King Lareth?" the count abruptly asked.

A smile. "No papers, sir. It is all here." She pointed to her head. "I think you are on the side of Sharsh in this affair."

"The Coradean resistance."

"So it is." Those who opposed the Imperial Union, who were sometimes being arrested and silenced. Galaro had heard the rumors and tried to ignore them. It was not his concern.

What did this woman, this Bela know? Names of leaders? Perhaps she carried a secret message to the king and his council.

"Yes," agreed Orgelo, "I wish this union no more than does Sharsh. I would guess you intend to head for Doram Pass."

She nodded. It was the obvious route. Of which any pursuers would be aware. Would they follow her that far?

"I could send a guard with you that far," began the count, "but my neighbors would not at all appreciate a troop of men crossing their lands."

"I can only try to make it, sir. If I had a horse I might elude any pursuit."

Galaro made a decision. "I've a better idea. You, Orgelo, send a small decoy group north. They can slip back at night later on, without even crossing your border. And Mistress Bela here can travel with my traders until we reach a place she can safely leave us."

"And how many more Crowns would you expect, sir?"

"Just the one you owe," came his gruff reply, "and one for the family of the man who died. You should have let us know we were in danger, woman."

She hung her head. "Yes, I should have, sir. I hoped I had cleanly escaped those who pursued. You shall have the two Crowns." She retrieved a purse from somewhere about her and produced the coins. Galaro wondered how much else wealth was in it.

He took the coins, nodded his head. "And, of course," he said, "if you travel as a trader you must work as a trader. No more malingering on the backs of wagons."

"Gladly. You have my word, Captain."

He smiled slightly at the title. She was already picking up the trader ways. That was to be expected of a spy, maybe.

"Oh, by the way, Sir Galaro," said Count Orgelo, "The exchange of money reminded me. Something came here for you—yes, here it is."

He pulled a folded paper from his desk. Inside were four Royals and a scrawled message. *This makes us even, sir, when it comes to cash, but I shall ever owe you for so much more.* It was sighed, *Godos.*

Galaro pouched the coins. "We'll roll away the day after tomorrow. Be ready."

~ ~ ~

"Jobareth's sister wrote this," she told Pol. "Erlana Nafal. I think parts of it are good. She was terribly nervous about asking me to look at it!"

"And to pass it on to me?" He leafed through quickly. Too quickly to actually read anything.

"Yes. And if you steal any of it, you will answer to me!"

He had stopped at a page. "This is a pretty decent song," he admitted. "I wonder if she has music for it." He looked up. "I have a good melody writer is she doesn't."

It had never occurred to her that Pol didn't write his own tunes. Jobareth had at least attempted; maybe his sister did too.

Pol put the pages aside. "You dress still as a bride," he remarked. That he meant it as at least a bit of jest she could tell. Pol jested much but could also be quite serious.

"I have decided to dress only in white henceforth, as my father did in black."

"Then, my wife," said Blen, "we'd best ride no more dirt roads."

"You will follow behind me with a little broom to keep me swept clean."

She could see from Pol's expression he was thinking about whether he could use that line. "But this gown is nothing like that stiff affair I wore yesterday." Encrusted with pearls and lavished with too much lace! She really should have kept an eye on Lady Lis. "I blame it entirely for my stumbling. It and the fact that you got in my way."

"We'd best be packing all your clothes, whatever color they be," Blen reminded her.

"Then you will be on your way tomorrow?"

"We will. A boat will take us downriver first and then we'll travel about a bit. Maybe go all the way to the sea."

"A good place to be when the weather gets warm," said Pol. "And to meet pirates."

"The only pirates I hope to see will be on the stage of our theater." She would always call it 'our' from now on. She considered Pol, that unsophisticated boy of a soldier she and her friends had adopted—so to speak—her partner now. But the theater would wear her name. The name of Viscountess Fachalana was a draw.

She would concern herself with no magics until they returned to Celatas. She would not open her father's villa. It could wait. Lareth and Doufan could manage to run Sharsh without them!

They had been told what she learned from the Partanacan wizard. That they could do with as they would. It would have done no good to mention the Asakian. Nor those enigmatic twins. What connection had they to her father? She could push all that aside for a while.

Blen had spread a map on the table. "Down to about here," he was telling Pol. "My folks' place is a little lower on the river and, um, Ildoravem—is that the right name?"

Fachalana nodded. She had decided to so rename the estate her father had left her.

"Ildoravem is here. There's a long used road right through the hills there." He squinted at the writing. "Oh, the Cave of Ghosts. I remember it."

"We shall have to visit and tell each other scary stories," she told him. But she had already lived through ones far scarier than the housemaids had told her as a little girl.

And she might be frightened by the stories to come, the ones she would write when she took up her powers again, went forth to free

230

her father, to learn who she herself truly was. But all that would wait.

All she cared about now was *now*. Now and the man she shared it with.

AFTERWORD

So we bring to a close the first Book of "Destiny's Daughter." There will be a second Book and, most likely, more to follow. "Destiny's Daughter" continues the stories of many of the characters in the four Books of "Donzalo's Destiny." Donzalo himself, however, has comfortably settled into a supporting role here and Lady Fachalana now has moved center stage. She likes it there.

By the way, for any who might have wondered about the money that changed hands in this book, five Royals are equal to one Crown, and both are coins of Sharsh.

www.ingramcontent.com/pod-product-compliance
Lightning Source LLC
Chambersburg PA
CBHW030329030726
47499CB00003B/706